SHERIFF OF BIG HAT

Center Point
Large Print

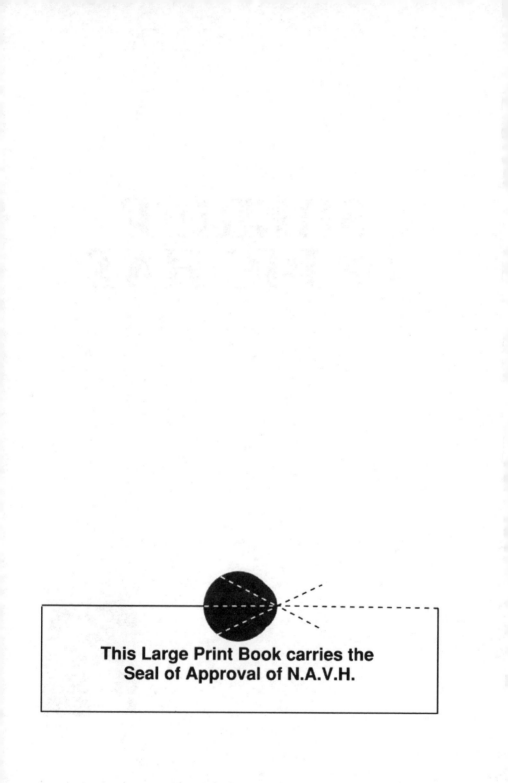

**This Large Print Book carries the
Seal of Approval of N.A.V.H.**

SHERIFF
OF BIG HAT

SHERIFF OF BIG HAT

Barry Cord

CENTER POINT LARGE PRINT
THORNDIKE, MAINE

This Center Point Large Print edition
is published in the year 2016 by arrangement with
Golden West Literary Agency.

First US edition: Arcadia House
Frist UK edition: Brown Watson

The text of this Large Print edition is unabridged.
In other aspects, this book may vary
from the original edition.
Printed in the United States of America
on permanent paper.
Set in 16-point Times New Roman type.

ISBN: 978-1-68324-181-2 (hardcover)
ISBN: 978-1-68324-185-0 (paperback)

Library of Congress Cataloging-in-Publication Data

Names: Cord, Barry, 1913–1983, author.
Title: Sheriff of Big Hat / Barry Cord.
Description: Center Point Large Print edition. | Thorndike, Maine :
Center Point Large Print, 2016.
Identifiers: LCCN 2016038556| ISBN 9781683241812 (hardcover : alk.
paper) |
  ISBN 9781683241850 (pbk. : alk. paper)
Subjects: LCSH: Large type books. | GSAFD: Western stories.
Classification: LCC PS3505.O6646 S525 2016 | DDC 813/.54—dc23
LC record available at https://lccn.loc.gov/2016038556

CHAPTER I

The sound of creaking saddle leather floated through the early morning grayness, stilling the sleepy whistle of a wren in the bushes off the trail. A broad-shouldered, narrow-hipped rider loomed up on the rimrock and became a black etching against the eastern sky. Another showed up on his left, like a shadow—and a moment later a giant figure eased up on his right.

The faint clang of a shod hoof on stone died out against the quiet. In the grayness a match flared as the first rider lighted a cigaret.

The Kid sucked in smoke. His gray eyes were on the vague cluster of buildings, like toy blocks, making a careless pattern on the long flat below them.

He said dryly, "That's it. That's Del Rio." He let smoke dribble out of his nose, and his lips twisted oddly as if the sound of the name were unpleasant.

The giant on his right shrugged. He sat heavily in the saddle of his huge gray stud, his blue eyes sleepy and seemingly disinterested. He had crisp red hair thinning on his brow and turning gray at the temples, and a trick of running two fingers of his right hand across the pale two-inch scar above his left eye.

Slowly he eased forward for a better look at the country below the rimrock.

In the north a hat-shaped butte dominated eroded wasteland. To the east rangeland ran to vague peaks that marked the sere, rocky Blackrocks. Southward, low ridges faded into the tangled *bosque* of the Rio Grande flatlands.

"So that's Del Rio?" The tall, spare-framed man on the Kid's left framed the question absently, as though he had been only half listening, his thoughts far away. He was an oldish man, his smallness accentuated by rounded shoulders and a caved-in posture. His long, bony face had a remote cast; the Kid had never seen him smile. He packed a doctor's instrument bag on the saddle behind him; he had once shown the Kid a medical degree from some Eastern college. That much the Kid knew about the "Doc"—nothing more.

The Doc suddenly roused from his slumped position over his saddle horn, as if realizing the end of a long trail was in sight. He said: "Let's see that note again, Kid."

The younger man unbuttoned the pocket of a black, dusty shirt, handed the older man an envelope. The message was written in a flowing hand on expensive linen paper.

"Ten thousand dollars is a lot of money," Doc commented, handing the letter back, "even for bucking a killer like Yaegar." He looked closely

8

at the youngster, frowning. "Think this Judge Miller can pay it?"

The Kid was looking down into the lightening valley. He seemed to ignore the Doc's question. But after a time he answered, "Yeah—he can pay it. He owns, or did own, the biggest ranch this side of the Blackrocks."

Jackson, the giant on the Kid's right, turned slowly, interest stirring in his blue eyes. "You sound like you knew this section, Kid. You been holding out on us?"

The Kid took the cigaret from between his lips and flipped it over the rim. The gesture was half impatient, half bitter.

"I was born in Del Rio. I was nineteen when I left town, a rope-anxious posse on my trail. My own father was in that posse."

He stopped with that. The early morning silence held the weight of things unspoken. His companions waited, but when the Kid eased back in his saddle they looked at one another and shrugged.

Jackson nodded, his voice indifferent. "We're splittin' up here then, like we planned. We'll ride into Del Rio by different trails an' we'll rendezvous in Pedro's Café Reale by sundown. That right, Kid?"

The Kid nodded.

The giant dropped a hand to ease the weight of the long-barreled heavy Frontier Colt jutting ominously from a snugged-down holster. But the Doc hesitated. He spoke slowly, picking his words.

"For me and Jackson this is just another job, Kid. We buck Yaegar and his bunch of gun-slicks—for ten thousand American pesos." He was watching the Kid's hard brown face. "But you have reasons for coming back here. Way back in Pasado, before we even got this note, you wanted to come to Del Rio. Why?"

The Kid was silent a long time. He was a hard man who had built a wall around himself. In the years the Doc had known him he had never been confidential about his past. He wasn't now.

He said: "Call it my personal business, Doc. Something I should have attended to long ago. Just call it that, and forget it."

The Doc frowned, not liking the Kid's answer. But he did not press him. Theirs was a loose alliance, held together casually, and it was an unspoken agreement between them that the past history of their lives remain a closed chapter.

Jackson smiled, with a peculiar twist of the lips that seemed to hold a brief, sardonic mirth. He said: "See you in Pedro's," to both of them. He eased his gray stud away, the sound of the animal's shod hoofs fading into the grayness that shrouded the trail.

The Doc remained hunched over his saddle, brooding. He was thinking of the five years they had ridden together; Jackson, the Kid and he. And he didn't even know the Kid's real name.

He studied the youngster, trying to fathom the thoughts behind the impassive features.

The Doc knew Jackson better than he knew the Kid. He had run into the redheaded giant on the old Mescalero trail one stormy winter night. Two drifters heading in the same direction. They had teamed up. Neither man had asked the other questions, nor tried to force himself into the privacy of the other's thoughts.

In the passing years the Doc had come to know the big man's violent swings of mood, the strength in those huge shoulders and gnarled yet nimble fingers, the deceptive quickness in that bulky body. He knew how the big man ate, slept, washed.

But of Jackson's life before that moment they had met on the Mescalero trail he knew nothing. Only one hint was vouchsafed in a question the big man often asked.

Along many trails, in many towns, Jackson had inquired casually about a man. A man named Red Becker. He had not found him.

They had picked up the Kid three years after the Mescalero trail meeting. They were crossing a corner of the Staked Plains when they found the youngster, a bullet wound festering in his thigh. He was dragging himself toward the hills. A mile before they had come upon the carcass of his horse.

The Doc nursed him back to health. When he was able to ride he rode with them. They didn't ask questions. The Kid volunteered nothing.

Gun-handy, grimly efficient and with a cynical eye on the law which, in those violent times, was often backed not by justice but by the unanswerable logic of the fastest gun, a reputation had grown around them. And a name—the Unholy Three.

Their guns were for hire to the highest bidder—they accomplished their job, took their pay, and drifted on.

So it had been for more than four years.

But Del Rio was going to prove different. The Doc felt it as he brooded. The Kid's past was in Del Rio.

He smiled sadly, thinking how little each of them knew about the other. Neither the Kid nor Jackson knew what had made of him a wanderer—nor could he guess what it was that had driven the Kid from Del Rio.

Now he watched the Kid, trying to fathom what lay behind the brown, impassive face. Finally he shrugged. It was the Kid's play, and he would handle it.

He swung the fidgety palomino he was riding away from the rim, echoed Jackson's "See you in Pedro's." He had the feeling the youngster hadn't heard him as he rode away.

CHAPTER II

Jackson Rode into Del Rio first—a big man with a sleepy slouch and two bone-handled guns tied low on his hips. He came in across the wooden bridge that spanned the almost dry river bed and swung west along the dusty trail that widened to become Del Rio's main street.

There was a long frame structure squatting on the west corner of the first cross-street. A dark-faced Yaqui Indian hunkered on his moccasined heels in the shade, smoking a brown paper cigaret. He watched Jackson ride past; then he straightened, shuffled into the wooden building.

A moment later a tall, hatchet-faced man with a brown calf-skin vest came out and stared at Jackson's broad back. He waited with frowning gaze until Jackson turned into Texas Square before going around to the back yard and mounting a saddled roan. He hurdled a low fence, crossed a littered lot and rode west, pushing the animal. . . .

Texas Square, once known as Plaza de Coronado, was the heart of Del Rio. It resembled an amphitheatre—a wide, dusty plaza encircled by two-story, double-deck verandas and a single towering three-decker frame and adobe building that was identified by a single word painted above the heavy oaken door: YAEGAR'S.

Jackson noted the legend with sleepy-eyed interest. His glance slid with only casual interest over the gunman taking things easy in a tipped-back chair on the wooden porch. A wide-brimmed hat shaded the man's heavy jowled face. The man needed a shave and a bath. A thin trickle of cigaret smoke seeped up under his hat.

Across from Yaegar's a low, dirty-gray adobe building had a sign that read: SHERIFF'S OFFICE. There were bullet holes in the sign.

A wiry man about the Doc's age was crossing the square to the law office. He stopped to appraise Jackson, eyeing the big man thoughtfully. He wore a star on his black vest and two guns, belts crossing, on his lean hips. His boots were scuffed and run over at the heels, and there was a bowed look about him that went beyond his bowed legs.

He looked at Jackson, and his casualness gave way to a bitter hostility that reached out across that hot square to slap Jackson in the face with its intensity. The big man stiffened and came up on his stirrups, alertness wiping the sleepiness from him.

But the gun-metal blue eyes left him, and the lawman continued across the square, shuffling with bowed head to the low adobe office.

Behind Jackson the silent figure on Yaegar's porch got to his feet. He took his burned-out cigaret butt from his mouth, spat shreds of tobacco into the street. A knowing smile rounded his lips as he shouldered the heavy door open and stepped inside.

Jackson felt this, as he had sensed the departure of the hatchet-faced man on the edge of town; sensed the loaded trap that was Del Rio. And he felt wariness crawl through him, tingle his spine.

He and the Doc and the Kid had run into some tough opposition before. But he was moody this afternoon, gray with the recurring torment of his thoughts, as he paced his cayuse toward the narrow Avenida de Sangre leading off Texas Square. He had these spells of depression, and they made him taciturn and as irritable as a hungry grizzly.

He felt the need of a drink, and suddenly he hated the idea of going to Pedro's Café Reale, hated the thought of the methodical plans they had laid.

A small saloon on the south side of Texas Square, shaded by a tall eucalyptus tree, caught his eye, and he nosed the gray up to the rail, dismounted, and went inside.

The three customers at the small bar edged over as he breasted the dark wood. He growled: "Rye," and tossed a gold eagle on the counter. He took the bottle and the glass and filled the glass, tossing the liquor down.

The bartender was a one-armed man with a sloppy face. He kept a towel bunched up on the bar, pretending to use it to wipe the counter top.

Under the towel was a snub-nosed .38. He was pretty handy getting to it when an emergency arose, and he could hit what he aimed at.

Jackson drank four straight before the liquor began to burn inside him. He pushed the bottle to one side then and asked the question he had asked in more than a hundred towns—asked with decreasing hope:

"Anyone here ever hear of a gent named Red Becker?"

The bartender put his hand on the towel. The three men further down the bar stopped talking. The room suddenly held the quality of an open powder keg with a man fumbling with a match by the open lid.

"Sure," a voice answered coolly. "You a friend of his?"

Jackson turned, like a tiger wheeling. In the half-darkness of a corner table a kid slowly got to his feet. A thin-faced youngster with straw hair and a button nose.

The room cleared behind Jackson as the big man strode over to the youngster. The boy held his ground, but he flinched nervously when Jackson loomed over him. Suddenly he lashed out with his right fist.

Jackson caught the hand before it reached his face. His fingers tightened and the blond puncher paled, his lips drawing back over his teeth.

Jackson's voice was like the dark, vicious mood riding him. "Where is Becker?"

The youngster stopped trying to get free. Sweat jeweled his forehead and upper lip. He grated: "Becker's out at the Dia—"

The rifle cracked sharply. Jackson felt the slug splat into the slim figure at the same moment. The boy jerked, and Jackson was like a jungle cat, cornered and seeking escape.

He was across the room before the youngster sagged to the floor, a gun sliding into his big fist. The rifle cracked once more, trying to target him as he moved. Lead gouged into the far adobe wall. Jackson shot twice at the figure he saw in the doorway and it vanished, swallowed in gunsmoke.

A dark raging mood was in the big man, and he hurdled an overturned table on his way to the door. He knew the killer might be waiting for him to come out; waiting with cocked rifle. But his rage was greater than his caution.

The Square was empty when he plunged out to the plank walk. Empty save for the restless horses tied up at the rails—and the wiry lawman who was coming across the sunbeaten plaza, walking slowly, like a man who didn't care what had happened, indifferent but impelled by duty to investigate.

Baffled, the big man hesitated. Then he remembered the youngster who had been about to tell him where he could find Red Becker—tell him what he had lived to find out for ten years.

He went back inside. But the tow-haired puncher was dead.

He was rising from the boy's body when the lawman came into the saloon. He shuffled leisurely over to him. There was no expression in the sheriff's lined, sunbaked features; he only looked old and tired.

Jackson faced him stiffly, expecting hostility. But the lawman's tone was mild. "What happened?"

Jackson growled his explanation. The bartender added: "That's the way it was, Judd. Lou started to tell the stranger about Becker when somebuddy killed him."

The sheriff appraised Jackson thoughtfully. "So you're looking for Red Becker?"

Jackson nodded. He didn't feel like answering questions, and strangely enough the sheriff didn't ask them.

"You'll find Becker in that building across the square," the sheriff said. He offered the information with no indication of interest. "In Yaegar's. I just saw him ride in."

Jackson glanced down at the dead puncher. "Then it wasn't Becker who shot the kid?"

"No." The sheriff did not elaborate. "Lou rode for the Big Hat. They're having trouble with the Diamond Cross outfit. Becker rides for the

Diamond Cross." He waited, not smiling, letting Jackson make of this what he would.

Jackson shrugged. The youngster's death did not touch him, nor the reason for it. He wheeled away from the lawman, bent without slowing his stride and scooped up his black hat. He jammed it on his head and paused in the doorway, practiced fingers replacing the spent shells in his fired Colt.

He had forgotten he was due to meet the Doc and the Kid at Pedro's; forgotten his carefully laid plans. All else was submerged beneath the turmoil inside him save the fact that Red Becker was in town, only one hundred and fifty yards away.

He crossed the square on foot, a big shambling man in the heat of the high-riding sun. And from a second floor window in Yaegar's a heavy, red-faced man watched him come, a nervous smile spreading thinly across his lips. . . .

Yaegar's door was of four-inch oak, but it swung in easily under the thrust of Jackson's palm. The big man's blind hate drove him to relax his caution. He padded to the long counter looming against the south wall. Sunlight streamed through the door he had left open. It made a long narrow path across the wide plank floor, lining the big man against the brightness of the empty Square.

The big room echoed hollowly to the scuff of Jackson's boots. A swamper, sweeping behind the bar, looked up. He was a small, pock-faced bum who had lost ambition early and now held life cheaply.

He leaned on his broom, staring with puckered lips at Jackson. The big man asked softly, too softly: "Where's Becker?"

The cued swamper waved toward stairs that led up to the open-railed balcony hanging over the middle of the big room. He spat into the sweepings as Jackson wheeled away.

The big man moved swiftly, his right hand heeling the butt of his Colt. He was five feet from the first step, and just opposite a closed door marked PRIVATE, when he heard a door close up on the balcony. A red-faced man, heavier than Jackson recalled, came to the railing. He was smiling, showing yellowed stumps of teeth.

"Looking for me, Jackson?"

Jackson heard the door sigh open at his side—the warning barely touched him as he jerked his Colt out and muzzled it upward. He retained a memory of a single shot that seemed to prolong itself, merge into a great roaring in his head before he fell into blackness. . . .

CHAPTER III

The Doc rode in from the south, skirting the Mission of San Pablo that looked down from a knoll on the town sprawled along the river. His small figure hunched broodingly over his saddle horn. There was no tension in him as he came into Del Rio. . . .

A woman and a child stopped to let him pass and sunlight, striking gold from the little girl's curly hair, struck a lost chord in him momentarily. For just an instant he allowed himself a look down the corridor of his past years, to a smal elm-shaded town where once he had been respected as Jonathan Taber, M.D.

He came out of his sombre reverie to find himself in Texas Square. Jackson's big gray stud, impatiently nudging the saloon rail across the plaza, immediately caught his attention.

The Doc had the brief, disturbing thought that Jackson was in trouble. But he kept riding, heading for the agreed meeting place.

The Avenida de Sangre was a narrow alley between high adobe walls. At the end of the old Spanish street stood Pedro's Cantina—a pretentious affair with a second story gallery running around three sides of the square building.

The Doc dropped his reins over the cross-pole,

surveyed the Diamond Cross brands on the slack-hipped cayuses nosing the rail and went inside.

The barroom was a gloomy place with a cool, earthy smell. There was no one behind the counter. At a rear table a mountainous Mexican with a bland moon face, a wisp of mustache and incongruously blue eyes stopped dealing with a grunt of impatience. The three other players craned curious necks. They looked like tough cowpokes who would be handier with a gun than a branding iron.

At the only other occupied table a slim young Mexican, gaudily dressed in green velvet charro jacket, and bell-bottomed, silver-ornamented trousers cinched at the waist by a bright red silk sash, was talking to a *señorita* with mischievous dark eyes.

The Doc made his way to the bar, planted a foot on the rail, and waited.

The huge man slapped his cards on the table, heaved out of his chair and came around the counter, a scowl on his face. "I'm Pedro," he said shortly. "What you havin', stranger?"

"Whiskey." The Doc slid a silver dollar between his fingers and tossed it on the counter.

The big man placed a bottle and a glass before him. "Serve yourself," he said briefly, and went back to the card game.

The Doc sipped his first drink. It was getting along in the afternoon. The Kid wasn't due in

Pedro's until sundown. He'd have several hours to kill.

He wondered what had happened to detain Jackson. He knew the big man's gray moods. He shrugged and finished his whiskey. Jackson was big enough to take care of himself.

Doc was pouring himself another drink when he became conscious of a pair of eyes studying him. He toyed with his glass before he turned, making the move appear natural. One of the card players dropped his gaze. He was a long beanpole with a scraggly brown mustache and a sad sort of face. The Doc tried to place him.

The hard jingle of spurs sounded flatly in the cool quiet. The batwings parted. A rangy, hard-bodied man with a hatchet face and a cigaret drooping from his thin lips came in, evidently looking for someone. He bounced a quick glance off the card players, held his gaze for a moment on Doc. Frowning, he paced to the table where the young Mexican was obviously trying to make time with the dark-eyed girl.

His voice held a rough edge. "Drinking again, Jose?"

Jose glanced over his shoulder. "Go away, Slim," he said carelessly.

Slim's lips crimped hard around his cigaret. He stepped around to the girl's side of the table, toed up a chair and sat in it, facing Jose. He leaned forward, ignoring the girl. The *señorita* sniffed.

He said coldly: "Lay off the drinking, Jose."

The card players stopped playing.

The easiness slipped from Jose; the quick humor faded from his face. Anger flushed dark on his cheeks. "Slim—no one tells Jose what to do!"

The slim man's voice did not raise. "*I'm* telling you! Lay off the drinking! You haven't got the head for it, and your tongue gets too loose." He glanced meaningly at the girl, who gave him a sullen look.

The Mexican sneered. "I talk when I please—and I drink when I want, Slim." He leaned across the table and prodded the rangy man's chest. "*Get out!*"

The Doc sensed rather than saw the change in Slim. The man didn't move, didn't lift his voice. "Jose," he grated softly. "I'm telling you for the last time. Lay off the drinking. Yaegar wants to see you when he gets back!"

Jose laughed contemptuously. "I don't take orders from you, Slim. If Yaegar wants me to quit drinking, let him come tell me, eh?" He looked at the girl. "No one—not even Yaegar—tells Jose Martinez y Castinado when to drink!"

Slim's leashed anger slipped free. "You'll take orders, you overdressed, cocky—"

The Mexican lunged across the table and backhanded the man across the mouth. Slim skidded out of his chair and Jose straightened, piling the table on top of the man, spoiling Slim's draw.

Carmelita screamed as Slim scrambled up, a Colt in his hand.

The Doc was out of bullet line and he didn't move. But his eyes widened at what followed.

He didn't see Jose draw—it was that smooth and fast. There were two shots—both of them from Jose's weapon. Slim collapsed across the over-turned table.

Jose kicked a chair aside and walked to the card players sitting with rigid immobility around their table. "Anyone here like to take up Slim's unfinished business?" His voice was thick, challenging.

No one did. A short, pale-eyed man said, choosing his words carefully, "Yaegar won't like this, Jose—" and then stiffened as the slim Mexican turned to him. "All right, all right," he added hastily. "I'm not buckin' yuh. I got more sense than Slim had. But Yaegar won't—"

"The blazes with Yaegar!" Jose spat. He was slim and deadly and sure of himself—and arrogant with that knowledge. "No one orders Jose. Remember that, Keene!"

Keene did not dispute this, nor did anyone else at the table have anything to say.

Jose's ornaments jingled as he turned to the girl. "Carmelita!" His voice was roughly commanding. Then his mood changed as swiftly

25

as it had flared up. His smile was boyish as he took the girl's arm. "You have the *guitara* upstairs, no? Come—I weel serenade your beauty where your ears alone will hear."

The girl laughed merrily as they went upstairs.

Pedro finally rose. He walked to the body and looked down at it, probing between yellowed teeth with a nail-sharpened matchstick. He spat out bits of wood. "Give me a hand, Hank?" he asked the man with the sad face. "We'll take Slim into the back room."

Hank got to his feet. The short man Jose had called Keene said softly: "Some day someone's gonna take that greaser down a peg. But I wouldn't want to be the man to try it."

The Doc poured himself another drink. Hank and Pedro came back into the room and the cantina owner straightened the furniture before returning to the game. The Doc drifted over.

"Friendly game?"

Pedro looked up. "Two bit limit. Feel lucky?"

Doc nodded. In his long black coat he often passed for a professional gambler.

Hank was dealing. He shuffled the deck, placed it in front of the Doc. "Cut," he said softly.

The Doc cut.

Hank was studying his hands. Then his gaze came up and he held it on the Doc's face. "I've seen you somewhere before," he said watchfully. "Where?"

Doc smiled. "It's yore memory," he reminded him. "You figure it out."

Hank nodded. He dealt abstractedly, obviously reaching back into his past.

Doc had openers. He slid two bits toward the center of the table and waited while the others made their play. Hank was frowning at his cards, not reading them. Finally he looked up, his eyes meeting the Doc's cold blue stare with sudden amusement.

"Gunsight!" he sneered. "Two years ago!"

He tossed his hand into the discards and got up, kicking his chair back. The Doc watched him leave without emotion. It was Pedro who broke the silence.

"Raise," he said succinctly.

CHAPTER IV

Standing aloof from Del Rio, on the same level as the Mission of San Pablo, stood the Miller house. It was a palatial dwelling. Once it had been the hacienda of Juan de Esperanza Martinez y Castinado, who had come north with De Vaca in search of Cibola's mythical golden cities and been rewarded by the King of Spain with a tract of land that ran from the Rio Grande to the Blackrocks, seventy miles away.

Old, solid, the converted Spanish house faced the arid hills—a touch of grandeur in a barren and still largely primitive land.

The Kid rode in along the old Mission Trail, and the shadow of the church tower was like a voice recalling incidents of his boyhood.

The high adobe wall of the patio hid him from view of the house as he curbed his mount. He sat in the shade of a huge cottonwood and lighted a brown paper cigaret, and there was no emotion in his hard brown face.

He had come home after six years, and somehow there was no quickening in him, no warm surge of expectancy. For the big house behind the wall held few comforting memories. And there was in him now not even hate—only a vague and bleak regret.

He finished his cigaret, discarded it. Then he drew his feet up under him, balanced himself momentarily on his saddle, and jumped. The thick branch he grasped creaked under his weight. He drew himself up, swung a leg over the limb, and paused.

There was no one in the patio. The sun slanted across untended flower beds. A fountain, guarded by yellowed marble saints, tinkled dreamily into a small pool. There were benches of stone along the ivy-covered old walls, and a huge eucalyptus spread its umbrella of protection in the middle of the private garden. The drone of insects was heavy, lending a veneer of peace and serenity to the big house. But it touched no responsive chord in the Kid.

Hitching himself along the thick branch, he made the top of the wall, swung quickly over, hung a moment by his hands, and dropped. He straightened immediately, turned swiftly, and from habit his right hand dropped to the Colt butt snugged against his hip.

Bees buzzed with single-minded intentness among the flowers.

The Kid paced swiftly to the flagstone terrace. Here he paused, glanced into the room behind the French windows. The man he had come to see was inside.

Some of the old bitterness was in him, making him look young and petulant as he pulled open the double doors that led into the library.

Judge Henry Miller slid a manicured hand into the open desk drawer for the Smith & Wesson .38 that reposed there. His move was instinctive, a reflex conditioned by years of caution.

The Kid said meagerly: "I wouldn't, Uncle Henry."

Judge Miller hesitated. There was twenty feet of space between him and the Kid—and six years! Recognition rocked him back in his chair. Then he came to his feet, hand outstretched. "Gary! Gary, my boy! Welcome home!"

The Kid pointedly ignored the outstretched hand.

Miller flushed, dropped his hand. But his heartiness persisted. "Come in, Gary—come in. I'll have Juan bring you a drink." He stepped back to the library wall and pulled on a long tasseled cord. Somewhere in the big house a bell tinkled.

He was a tall, patrician-looking man of about forty with graying temples, a well-trimmed mustache, a small goatee. His spare figure was clad in a richly embroidered velvet coat. He had always, the Kid remembered, affected the dress and the manners of the Spanish dons who had preceded the Millers in this big house. But the

Kid knew, too, that the man's courtliness cloaked a calculating and ruthless nature, and it made the man's affability sound counterfeit to his ears.

"Tell me about yourself, Gary." His uncle smiled, waving him to a chair. "How have you been these past years?"

Gary couldn't hold back a faint sneer. *You've got a pretty good idea how they've been!* he thought bitterly. *You were here when I left Del Rio.*

But he didn't voice his thoughts. He said instead: "It has been a long time." Involuntarily he glanced up to twin oil portraits in ornate gilt frames hung on the wall behind the big mahogany desk.

One was of a gay young woman he had never known save by that painting. His mother. The other was a stern-mouthed man he had known well. His father.

Both were dead.

"I don't think you've forgotten that I'm still wanted in Del Rio for murder," he said dryly.

The older man waved a hand in sharp dismissal. "I never believed you killed Bob," he said quickly. "You should know that, Gary. I tried to talk sense into your father's head that night. But you know how he was. Once he got something in his head, he was stubborn as a desert burro. He—"

"Helped organize the posse that chased me out of town," the Kid finished. He turned as an old

Mexican shuffled into the room. Juan was old and nearsighted and he didn't recognize the lean stranger in the library. Henry Miller gave an order in Spanish, and Juan disappeared.

"I want the straight of it," Gary said quietly. "How did Father die?"

Judge Miller walked to the patio windows and stared into the garden.

"I heard it was Yaegar who killed him," the Kid pressed. "Is that right?"

His uncle turned. "I don't know," he answered. His face was sober and he seemed tired. "I really don't know," he repeated. "I was down in Laredo when the trouble started. I—we—" He hesitated, then looked Gary squarely in the eye. "You might as well know," he added quietly, "your father and I quarreled shortly after you left. I packed up and took the stage to Laredo. I didn't intend ever to come back."

He made a small, resigned gesture with his shoulders. "I was determined to stay away. I hung out my law shingle and started looking for clients." He smiled briefly. "I was down there less than two years when I heard that Yaegar had crossed the Border and bought out Salters' old place in the Blackrocks. He filed a brand and gathered around him some of the worst killers this side of the Mexican line. Men like Slim Trevor, Red Becker, Sam Insted, Texas Jack."

The Kid nodded. He had heard these names

before, and he knew their reputations. He had known what he would be bucking before he decided to come back.

The older man continued soberly, "Yaegar declared war on the Big Hat shortly after he got entrenched up in the hills. He shoved your father's brand out of the Blackrocks, killed off most of your father's best riders. I got a note from your father, and came back a month before he was killed. . . ."

Juan entered, silent-footed, leaving a tray on the desk. Judge Miller poured imported Bourbon into two glasses.

"I was here, waiting for your father, when he was killed. He and Sheriff Judd Vestry had ridden out early that morning to see Blake, your father's foreman at the Big Hat ranchhouse. He rode back alone that night, with a knife in his back. How he lived long enough to reach the house I'll never know. He was unconscious when I pulled him from saddle. He never even opened his eyes."

Gary Miller listened without visible emotion. He had never gotten along with his father, but as he listened to his uncle talk his mind ran back over the years. And he knew the fault had been his as much as the older man's. He had been a wild kid, hard to handle; a stubborn kid with a tendency to insolence. And the elder Miller, a hard and dominant man without his wife to soften him, had reined Gary in too hard.

The Kid felt regret now, and because it was too late to do anything about a life lived, anger ran a bitter course through him. He had left things unfinished in this town when, as a frightened, confused boy, he had let a posse chase him away and thereby confirmed to those behind the fact of his guilt.

This knowledge was suddenly clear and hard in him as he reached inside his shirt pocket and drew out a letter Judge Miller had mailed to the men known blasphemously or reverently, as the case might be, as The Unholy Three.

His uncle took the letter without a word. Then his fist clenched convulsively. "You're one of them?" he asked incredulously. *"You're the Kid!"*

Gary nodded with bitter irony. "The brand was on me a long time ago—I tried to live up to it."

Judge Miller shook his head. "And I thought you had come back because you had learned of your father's death, because you found out that the Big Hat was in trouble—" He left the remark hanging in mid-air, as though it were now of little importance.

"Why did you come back?"

"You hired us," the Kid reminded him bleakly.

Miller frowned. His shrug indicated his reluctant acceptance of this fact. "I had no idea where you were," he said tiredly. "When you left

Del Rio you vanished—as though you had never existed. I came back to help your father—I remained to do what I could with the Big Hat. But—" he turned away from Gary, looked out into the sunlit patio—"I can't buck Yaegar. Neither can Blake, nor the men still working for us at the Big Hat. I was desperate. So I sent a letter to men who had quite a reputation along the Border—men who were willing to use their guns for pay."

He turned to face Gary, his lips curling stiffly. "Men like you, Gary." His voice was suddenly quiet with the acceptance of this lean stranger who had come back to Del Rio. "What do you want to know?"

The Kid shrugged. "What will we be bucking?"

"Yaegar," the older man answered. "He bosses the Diamond Cross, a hole-in-the-hills spread stocked with beef from across the Mexican border. His cattle graze on grass that belonged to your father. Just a few weeks ago he bought out the old Palacio Verde and moved into town. It's sort of a headquarters for his men when they're in Del Rio." He turned abruptly and walked back to his desk. Lifting a corner of his blotter, he slid a slip of paper out, held it up to the Kid.

"I made this list out to hand to the men I was hiring. It's a list of the top men with Yaegar. Get those men and you break the power of the outfit—the wolves that are harrying the Big Hat will break up and scatter."

The Kid read the names without expression. Then he folded the slip, tucked it into his pocket. He asked bleakly: "Is Judd Vestry still wearing a badge in Del Rio?"

"He's wearing Yaegar's badge," his uncle answered acidly. "And his two deputies are Yaegar's riders." The Judge's lips curled with distaste. "Judd did a lot of talking in the old days about law and order. He was your father's friend, until Yaegar came back. Then he turned—like they all did—"

The Kid said softly, not waiting to hear the rest of what his uncle had to say, "I'll be seeing you later."

"Wait!" Miller came up to him. "The Big Hat's yours, Gary. What do you intend doing with it?"

"Save what's left of it," the Kid answered levelly. He stepped to the patio windows, nodded coldly and went out.

CHAPTER V

Gary Miller rode down the old Mission Trail to Del Rio with the sun fading on his back. The town sprawled out before him—an L-shaped cluster of adobes along the bend of the river. A collection of sun-baked mud huts, squalid and cramped and overrun by half-naked brown children, chickens, goats and chattering women who fell silent as he rode through the narrow streets of the Mexican quarter. . . .

Gary was remembering these streets when, as a youngster, he had stolen from his bedroom under the light of a sickle moon and gone prowling through the alleyways with Bob Vestry and young Jose Castinado. They had been three of a kind then, he and the sheriff's son and slim, dark Jose whose forebears had owned the vast acres that now made up the Big Hat. Jose Castinado, whose father had worked for the Millers as a stable hand. . . .

The Kid had been wild then. He had changed little since. He felt the old unrest now—and he tried to lay a mental finger on just what it was that had brought him back to Del Rio.

It was more than his uncle's letter asking for gun help, more compelling even than the desire to know how his father had died.

Brown pigtails bobbing on a blue cotton shirt, blue-gray eyes that laughed easily, a freckled, pug-nosed face that could pucker with serious intent.

The stuff of dreams, these memories of Ann Vestry, coming at odd times to make him restless, drawing him back to Del Rio. . . .

He didn't know if Ann believed he had killed her brother Bob. He knew old Judd did. The sheriff had looked upon him as a wild kid who would come to no good. He had tried to keep Bob away from him, and when young Vestry had been killed the lawman had not stopped to weigh the evidence. Bob had been his only son, and old Judd had taken a fierce pride in the boy.

Gary recalled that night, how it had happened.

He had slipped out of his room, over the adobe wall, and made his way down to Del Rio. He and his father had quarreled again that morning, and he had been bitter and determined to run away. Bob Vestry had arranged to meet him in Vestry Square, and Jose was to join them later. Together they planned to head east and join the Texas Rangers.

He and Bob had gone to Pedro's Cantina Reale—they had gone there before—to wait for Jose. They bought a bottle of whiskey and went upstairs to one of the private rooms. Gary drank a lot and raged against his father's tyranny. Young Bob had tried to quiet him. Then the shot had come through the open window.

It was all rather blurred to Gary. The suddenness of the shot and the liquor had stupefied him. When he recovered sufficiently to move, he had stumbled to the window, and fired at a shadow he barely saw around a corner of the second floor veranda.

Bob was dead when he returned and bent over him. He heard voices coming up the stairs, and he reacted like a scared kid. He had climbed out the window, shinnied down a veranda support, and run home.

The sheriff had come for him that night. From his room overlooking the yard Gary had seen him ride up. His father had gone out to meet Judd, and the shred of conversation that had passed between them lingered in Gary's memory like acid in a wound.

"Thet darned kid!" his father had exploded. "He's gone too far this time, Judd—too far! Murder! I hope you see that he swings for it."

Gary had not waited to overhear more. He slipped out the back way, circled around to the front gate, and while the sheriff was inside the house, mounted the lawman's cayuse. And that was the way he had left Del Rio, six years ago. . . .

He was passing Yaegar's now, and he shrugged off the old memories. *Yaegar!* All over the Southwest that name was whispered in connection with a gun skill that was legend.

Where did the law stand in this fight between

the Big Hat and Yaegar's Diamond Cross? Where did Judd Vestry stand in this?

Gary remembered the lawman as a fighter. He had admired the lean, guntoting sheriff more than he had his father. He had even tried to pattern himself after the man. Somehow the picture his uncle had given him of the sheriff did not fit.

He had to know first, before he joined the Doc and Jackson. He had to know where the law stood.

The roan tossed its head as he swung it down a side street. He rode down an old cobbled alley and swung west toward Texas Square. A block from the law office he dismounted, tied the roan to a sagging board fence, and went forward on foot.

He knew this town by instinct, the back yards as well as the main thoroughfare. He hurdled a low adobe wall and walked swiftly to the back door of the law office.

A stable cast its long shadow across the small yard; a horse stamped uneasily in its stall. Flies buzzed over the manure pile.

Gary knocked on the door with the butt of his Colt.

A chair scraped inside the law office. Boots made a dragging sound on worn flooring.

The door started to open, and the Kid stepped up and shoved his shoulder against it. It held for an instant, then swung in, and the Kid was inside, kicking it shut behind him, his Colt levelling in his fist.

The sheriff, off balance, dropped his left hand in a clumsy move for his holstered gun. The Kid moved in and twisted the weapon from him and was surprised at the ease with which he accomplished it. He thrust the gun inside his belt, reached around and slid the sheriff's other weapon from holster.

He had moved fast, but still surprise lingered in him. It had been too easy.

He said harshly: "Relax, Judd. I want to talk to you."

The sheriff faced him, hunch-shouldered and bitter, and the thought came to Gary Miller that the years had broken Judd. He was seeing a small man with pale eyes in a seamed, bitter face—a smaller man than he remembered.

He was looking at Gary and he didn't know the Kid. "I don't know what yo're after, stranger," he said sharply. "The jail's empty—"

"Maybe that's what I'm after," Gary said bleakly. "I want to know why it's empty, Judd. I want to know what you're doing about Yaegar."

The old sheriff's head came up, and a pale blue flame flickered in his eyes. "Gary Miller." He snarled the name as recognition twisted through him. He lunged for the younger man, ignoring the levelled Colt.

The Kid hit him. He hated to do it. The lawman went down on his face.

Someone who had been dozing on the front porch came awake at the sound of Judd's fall. Chair legs thudded. Boots scuffed. A surly voice inquired: "Judd, what's going on in there?"

The Kid tossed the sheriff's guns on a cot by the wall as he stepped swiftly for the front door. The sheriff was stirring. He pushed himself up to his hands and knees and shook his head. "Baker!" he called thickly. "Look out—"

Baker was halfway inside, dragging at his gun, when the Kid brought the side of his Colt down on his head. Baker slumped. The Kid dragged his limp body inside and heeled the door shut.

Judd had regained his feet. His eyes focused on a gun rack across the room and he made a stumbling run for it.

The Kid beat him to it. He caught the sheriff's wrists, swung him around, jammed him against the desk. The lawman struggled like a man gone mad. And then, abruptly, he slumped, the strength going out of him, leaving him limp.

The Kid stepped back, glanced at Baker. The deputy was out cold.

Judd's breathing sounded harshly in the office. But his eyes were bright on Gary, alive with a hate that had fed itself through the years.

"What—do—you—want?" he gasped. "Why did—you come back?"

"To do what you should have done long ago," Gary answered. "Clean up Del Rio."

The old sheriff sneered. "That's big talk from a wild kid who killed my boy in a drunken brawl six years ago."

"You believe that, don't you?" Gary asked grimly.

"I never doubted it," the lawman grated. "I tried to keep Bob away from you. But he was a kid and he thought more of you than he did of me." Rage came up to choke Judd. "Why did you come back?"

"To get Yaegar!" the Kid snapped. "To find out who killed my father. And to see Ann!"

"Ann!" The sheriff's mouth pinched harshly; then suddenly he laughed. It was a short, ugly sound. "You sniveling fool! I'd kill her before—"

"Before what?" Gary demanded harshly. "What right have you to judge me? Where do you stand between Yaegar and the Big Hat? You were my father's friend—but you sold him out. When you did that you sold out that badge you're wearing!"

He stepped to the desk, took the keys that hung from a hook, and jerked a thumb toward an empty cell. "I'm taking over, Judd."

He paced to the cell, unlocked it. "Get in!" he snapped.

The sheriff glanced at Baker, who was just beginning to stir. His gaze moved to the Colts on the cot.

"Don't try it!" Gary warned bleakly.

The sheriff walked into the cell. Gary reached out as Judd passed and ripped the badge from the older man's vest. "You won't be needing this," he said. He locked the door after the bitter old man.

Baker was still half unconscious when Gary dragged him into another cell and plopped him on a straw mattress. He was coming out, locking the door, when the front door opened.

Gary whirled, his Colt flipping up. But a miracle of quick thinking kept him from firing.

The girl in the doorway stood rooted, staring at him, surprised recognition wiping the shock from her eyes.

"Gary Miller," she said.

He nodded, feeling tongue-tied after the long years of expectancy. He had planned a less abrupt meeting and words to bridge that gap of six years.

Ann Vestry had not grown taller, but she had filled out, and there was a woman's mature appraisal in her gray eyes. Some of the bitterness that marked her father had touched Ann. The lightness of her glance, the teasing quirk of her lips were memories he had carried with him; they were not part of this sober, tight-mouthed woman.

"Hello, Ann." The words were spoken with wooden lips.

She looked past him to Judd Vestry standing by

the cell door. She was dressed in a brown silk traveling dress that made her look older than her years, and she held a small embroidered bag in her hand.

Judd's lips tightened and he turned his face away. Ann's shoulders stiffened slightly.

Gary repeated his greeting. "It's been a long time, Ann—"

Her eyes were a stony gray, meeting his. "Mrs. Sigleman," she said coolly. She nodded slightly. "It has been longer than you think, Gary!"

He stood wide on his feet, absorbing this shock. "Congratulations," he said softly.

"You're more than a year late," she said coldly. "What brought you back to Del Rio?"

Standing there, he saw the boy he had been die—and he couldn't tell her.

He said instead: "Money."

She laughed understandingly. "I heard you were coming back because of your father. How silly! You hated him when I knew you—and you're not the type to grow sentimental, Gary!"

How little she knew him, he thought. He looked at her, trying to probe beneath her shell of bitter self-sufficiency.

Judd's voice came between them, thickly commanding. "Ann—get out of here!"

The girl looked past Gary, her eyes softening. "Dad—I'm leaving town. I came to say goodbye!"

Judd didn't say anything. He stood against the

door, and he didn't move. After a long moment Ann turned to Gary.

"I never believed you killed Bob," she said.

He nodded slightly. All he had wanted to say was bottled up inside him, and he no longer cared about Del Rio or what happened to the Big Hat. Nor did it seem to matter now what Ann Vestry—Ann Sigleman, he remembered—thought about Bob's death.

"Thank you," he said. His voice was dry.

"Let Dad out of that cell," she said. "He won't bother you, Gary."

He smiled at that.

Ann's eyes went out to that silent, bitter figure. "Tell him, Dad. Tell him the truth. Tell him why you haven't fought Yaegar—"

"He told me!" Gary snapped. "He's Yaegar's man!" A sudden deep resentment overwhelmed him—a resentment at being betrayed, first by a man he had idolized, now by a girl he had idealized.

He felt the sharp edges of Judd's star bite into his palm as he clenched his fist and looked down at that metal symbol of law and order.

He dropped Judd's star into his pocket and moved toward the door.

Ann's voice was sharp. "Gary—you don't know!"

He didn't stop. He heard her quick gasp, the swift patter of her feet. He had his hand on the knob when her voice reached him, like the flick of a whip. "Gary—wait!"

He turned his head. She was standing by the cot, one of her father's Colts in her hand. The hammer was cocked.

Gary stared at her for a long moment. Then he turned and pulled the door open and stepped out.

Behind him Ann sank down onto the cot and began to cry, softly—without tears.

CHAPTER VI

Daylight faded against the windows of the law office. Judd Vestry pressed against the cell bars, a small and bitter man, staring past the girl slumped on the cot. In the next cell Baker began to curse.

"Ann!" The sheriff's voice was urgent. He called again, impatience rising in his voice.

The girl finally looked up. She met his eyes, and in that moment she felt small and alone—and vulnerable.

"Ann!" Judd called sharply. "Get me out of here!"

The girl took in a deep breath. "Is that all you want of me, Dad?"

Judd's mouth went hard. "This is no time to bring up old arguments, Ann. You know how I feel. You knew how I felt when you disregarded me and married Mort Sigleman."

Ann rose. She still held one of Judd's Colts in her hand. "You didn't want me to marry Mort," she admitted. Her voice was dull, hurt. "You didn't want me to do anything. After Bob died you didn't care what happened to me. You treated me as though I didn't exist." She laughed shortly. "I had to do something, I guess. I had to show you I mattered, too. That's why I married Mort."

"He was no good!" Judd said harshly. "He was a gambler, a card sharp—a tinhorn!"

"He wanted me," Ann said stiffly. "He made me feel I was somebody—"

"He worked for Yaegar!" the sheriff reminded her coldly.

"One of Yaegar's gunmen killed him!" Ann said. She turned away in the darkening room, faced the window. "He stood up for me against them when they wanted to use me to force you to take Yaegar's side against the Big Hat. He had that much decency, Dad—something you never saw in him. And they killed him!" Her voice held a thin note of uncertainty, of wonder. "I was married to Mort Sigleman for one week. I was a widow the next."

Judd's face was stony. "Ann! Get me out of here!"

She turned, her laughter breaking harshly in that shadow-filled room. "Why? Why should I turn you loose?"

His eyes glared at her. "You know why, Ann. He's here! The man who killed Bob! I've waited for him for six years—"

"Gary didn't kill Bob!" Ann said. Her voice was flat. "I've never believed he shot Bob!"

Judd's fingers curled around the bars. "Ann!" he pleaded harshly. "Let me out of here! Do this one thing before you take that stage tonight. Get me out of here!"

She shook her head. "I'm not leaving tonight." She smiled at the look in Judd's face. "It was a shock, seeing Gary this afternoon. I never expected to see him again." Her voice dropped, as if she were reminiscing—talking to herself and wondering. "He was Bob's friend, Dad. They were together a lot. He and Bob and Jose. I was just a girl with pigtails. But he was my hero. You didn't know that, did you, Dad? You were always too busy to notice me—too busy checking on Bob—"

Judd wasn't looking at her. He was staring at the door, his lined face bitter, frustrated—unheeding.

"I don't know why Gary Miller came back," Ann continued. "Maybe it was for money—for what the Big Hat can give him. But seeing him again reminded me that I, too, was running away. From what, Dad?" She looked at him, her voice earnest. "I've done nothing to be ashamed of. I married a man who was a gambler. But he was killed before I knew I was married—"

Judd's snort cut her short. He turned away from her, his back stiff and unyielding.

Ann waited a few moments. Then she turned, tossed the Colt on the cot. As the door closed behind her she heard Baker's hoarse voice, muted through the panels. He was calling for help.

Gary Miller walked three long blocks in the deepening dusk before he became aware of his surroundings. He was in the Mexican quarter, a section of squalid mud huts and narrow alleys, and the smell of garlic and chile was strong in the warm air.

He stopped, and Gary placed himself. Calle del Norte—North Street. The alley ran to a big arroyo at the back of town and from there to the river. Many times had he come into Del Rio this way, running lightfooted and eager to a rendezvous with Jose and Bob Vestry. Three wild kids who had prowled the town and the country around, absorbing the smells and the lore of this border land.

How often had he heard Jose talk of the land of his fathers, the big Castinado land grant which had become the Big Hat. How often had he promised Jose and Bob that they would one day be his partners and run the Big Hat together.

Where was Jose now?

He reached into his shirt pocket for the makings, and while his fingers fashioned a cigaret his eyes probed the dusk, recalling that he had an appointment at Pedro's and that it was past sundown.

He searched in his pants pockets for a match, and his fingers met the cold steel of Judd's star. It reminded him he still had a job to do. He was responsible for the Doc and Jackson being here. Even now they were waiting for him. . . .

A hard smile edged his lips. The law was a

mockery here—had been for some time. Maybe it was time someone made this piece of metal mean something in the Blackrocks!

He lifted his hand and pinned it to his shirt pocket. Then he turned and made his way to the Avenida de Sangre—to Pedro's!

He paused just inside the cantina's swinging doors, conscious of the eyes that focused on the badge on his shirt.

The cantina had not changed in the interval he had been away. Nor had Pedro. The huge saloon-man was standing behind his bar, tending to a half-dozen customers, and his glance at the Kid was cursory. Strangers were not uncommon in his place, and evidently the past six years had wrought changes in Gary Miller that fooled Pedro.

The Doc was sitting in a card game at a corner table. His glance lifted to meet the Kid's, but he showed no sign of recognition. Jackson was not present. That fact disturbed Gary as he walked to the bar. He knew the big man's moods, and he sensed that something had gone wrong.

He breasted the bar close to where stairs led to the second floor. He was acutely aware of them, seeing in his mind the two kids who had gone up those stairs six years ago. He had nursed a hunch that Pedro knew what had happened that night. Knew who it was who had followed him and Bob and waited by that open veranda window. When he had more time, he reflected coldly, he was going to ask Pedro.

A lanky man with a low-slung gun and a cigar stub in a corner of his mouth turned from the bar as the Kid came up to foot the brass rail. He had tawny hair to match close-set eyes, and he looked Gary over with a slow, insolent regard.

"Badges are mighty unpopular in this town, stranger," he said. He had a nasal, high-pitched voice that grated on Gary's ear. "You aimin' to keep wearin' that piece of tin?"

The Kid faced him, setting himself for the trouble that was coming. This was Sam Insted. He recognized the Tombstone killer from descriptions he had seen on several county posters.

He said, "Yeah—I'm aiming to make it popular in town." Judd's twisted features rose up before him, and suddenly a bitter impatience drove him. "You objecting?"

The men flanking them at the rail edged away in a swift flurry of movement. Pedro, from behind the bar, said sharply: "Sam—no trouble! Not in here! I—"

"Shut up!" Sam growled. He did not take his eyes from Gary. "I don't like badges," he sneered, "especially when a tinhorn from nowhere comes in here wearin' one like he thinks it means somethin'. I aim to take it off an' teach him—"

The Kid slapped him across the face while the gunman was still talking.

The palm of his hand spread the cigar stub across Sam's face. For a split-instant the Tombstone killer was off balance, the shreds of tobacco on his face making him look foolish.

Then he reached for his Colt.

The Kid's .45 jammed its steel muzzle into his stomach before he cleared leather. Sam wrapped his long body around it, the breath whooshing out of him. The Kid clubbed him with the side of his Colt alongside his head.

Sam folded himself in a neat heap by the brass cuspidor at Gary's feet. The Kid whirled, his Colt backing the blazing challenge in his eyes. "Any other hombre in here who doesn't like this badge step up and say so!"

There was a most unusual silence.

Pedro eased his huge bulk against the back bar shelves. He was staring at the Kid, trying to pin down the identity of that lithe, dusty figure, the hard brown face, the lick of brown hair that came down over one cold blue eye.

He asked, surprised: "You the new sheriff?"

"New and self-appointed!" the Kid answered coldly. "And I'm setting up a few new regulations as of today. One of them is a warning to all Yaegar riders. Get out of Del Rio—and stay out!"

"All of them?" a voice asked softly, slurring the words. "All of them, Gary Meeler?"

• • •

The Kid eased his back against the bar and looked for the voice that had recognized him. He found it in the man who had come catlike down the stairs. The man who was now waiting on the landing where the stairs hooked and went up out of sight to the floor above.

"Jose!" he said, and memory fitted that gaudily dressed figure into the pattern of his youth. It was the swaggering bitter-tongued *muchacho* who had never forgotten that he was a Castinado.

Jose moved down the stairs, one hand on the railing. He was quite drunk. But a sense of drama was high in Jose, and he had always played to an audience. He was a Castinado, of proud heritage, and his arrogance, Gary saw, had crystallized around a deadly gun skill.

"You remember, no?" Jose asked thickly. "Jose Martinez y Castinado! The leetle ragged *muchacho* raised by Padre Tomas. You remember, Gary?"

Gary remembered. Jose, the boy who had scorned Miller's helping hand when his father was killed in a stampede of Miller cattle. His mother dead, Jose had been left an orphan—and kindly old Padre Tomas had taken him in. But neither the soft words of the *padre*, nor the influence of the cross he had grown up under, had changed this kid who would always remember that his father had been a Castinado—and that the Castinados had once owned the Miller acres.

He was young, a year younger than Gary—but there was no youth in either of them now. Watching Jose, Gary had the dismal feeling that words would not deter this man from his course. As a boy, Jose had talked of getting back the Miller *rancho*—as a man he would try to take it.

"I wait for you seex years," Jose said. He had reached the floor, and now he stopped, less than six feet from the bar. In all that room there was no other movement, no other sound. . . .

"I knew you would come back to Del Rio," Jose went on. "You are a Meeler—and I am the last of the Castinados!"

It was melodrama, drawn out for the sake of his audience. But Gary knew it was Jose's way.

"You one of Yaegar's men?" he asked curtly.

"I work for Yaegar sometimes," Jose admitted. "Together we join to smash the Beeg Hat—"

"No!" Gary cut in bleakly. "Neither you nor Yaegar will smash the Big Hat, Jose!"

Jose laughed. "You theenk we deed not know, huh? About the Unholy Three?" He nodded as the Kid's eyes narrowed. "*Si*, Gary—we knew you were comin'." He glanced at the table where the Doc was sitting, silent and watchful. "That ees why yore beeg *compadre*, Jackson, ees not here. *Si*—we knew—"

He lifted a hand to brush hair out of his eyes, and his dark face went ugly with purpose. He had the attention of his audience, and it was time for his big scene. "Eet was Yaegar's idea," he sneered. "Weeth you out of the way, the Beeg Hat ees hees. But Yaegar ees a fool, too—not even he weel take over the land of the Castinados!"

"You were always sure of that, Jose—weren't you?" Gary asked softly. He knew what he had to do, and he wondered if he was fast enough. There had always been an animal quickness in Jose—a restless energy that nagged at his muscles, sent him prowling the alleys of Del Rio long ago. . . . "Even when you were a kid," he reminded him grimly, "I used to have to whip you twice a week—"

He drew and fired as Jose went for his gun. Even drunk, Jose was fast; fast enough to beat Gary. His slug took a slice of shirt and skin from Gary's left arm, slashed a deep groove across the bar top, and put gray hair in Pedro's thick thatch as it thunked into the back wall an inch from the bar owner.

Gary's shots were luckier. The Kid did not fool himself. He had tried for Jose's gun arm, not wanting to kill this man he had once called friend. His first shot grazed the back of Jose's gun hand; his second broke his arm just above the elbow.

Jose dropped his gun. He was bent over in a half-crouch, and his dark eyes held the shock of pain. Then he lost his head. He lunged for Gary with his empty left hand clawing for Gary's throat, his right dangling useless by his side.

Gary slugged him. Jose fell against him, his fingers sliding down Gary's shirt front. He went down slowly, his eyes rolling back, the whites showing, glinting in the smoky lamplight.

Across the room Doc had come to his feet, his Colt holding two very surprised Yaegar men stiff and unmoving at their places at the card table.

The Kid stood over Jose's unconscious form. A board creaked on the steps and he whirled, his Colt challenging the girl who had tiptoed down to the landing. She shrank back against the wall, a dim figure in the shadows.

Gary's voice was sharp. "Who are you?"

"Carmelita!" The girl shook her mass of black hair, looped earrings flashing. Her voice held a muted defiance. "I tol' Jose not to come downstairs. I tol' him—"

"Take care of him," Gary interrupted coldly. "He's going to need you when he comes to!"

He stepped away from Jose. Sam Insted was stirring, groaning softly. Gary bent over him, took his gun and jammed it inside his belt. He turned to Pedro, standing motionless against the backbar.

"You used to run a clean place here," he said coldly. "I'll give you a chance to continue it. But the next time I find a Yaegar man in here, I'm closing it!"

Pedro didn't say anything.

Gary reached down and grabbed Sam by his

collar. The gunman was trying to get to his feet. His face was like muddy coffee. The Kid's yank helped him up. Sam swayed, reached out for the bar to steady himself.

Gary said: "We're going for a walk, Sam, across the square."

Sam's mouth twisted in a barely audible curse. He dropped his hand to his empty holster, let it fall by his side.

Gary grinned bleakly. "Walk!"

Sam stumbled away from the bar. He walked bent over, trying to keep his stomach from turning over. There was no fight left in him.

Gary paused by Doc's side. "Take their irons," he instructed shortly. "We're fillin' a couple of cells tonight."

Doc nodded. He glanced briefly at Jose's unmoving figure, remembering the deadliness of the slim man. And a gray foreboding disturbed him. The Kid was making a mistake letting Jose live!

The two men at the card table rose, fell in behind Sam Insted. They didn't look back. They pushed out through the slatted doors, moving carefully, like men walking on eggs. . . .

CHAPTER VII

The shadows were thick in Texas Square. Around the edges of the big plaza lamplight made patterns in the dust. The wind blew up from the south, from the Mexican quarter, bringing the sound of a crying child and the soft plucking of a guitar. . . .

The stage came in at a hard run from Pottsville to the north. It was running empty, bringing the mail on this leg of its run to El Paso. It expected to pick up three passengers in Del Rio and more mail.

Gary Miller watched it roll past. He thought of Ann Vestry—Sigleman, he remembered— She would be leaving on this stage. With whom? Her husband? He had found out nothing about her, except that she was married.

He felt the Doc's presence by his side as they started across the square to the sheriff's office. The older man's silence lay like a wall between them.

They crossed the square behind the three Yaegar gunmen and stepped up to the awninged walk, stopping before the darkened law office. Several men were clustered about the door. They moved away as Gary and his prisoners loomed up.

Gary asked sharply: "Looking for the sheriff?"

The shadowy men backed away. One of them

shook his head. "We been hearing someone in there yelling for help—" He gasped, recognizing the lanky Yaegar gunman sagging against the door. "Sam Insted!" He backed away hurriedly. His movement was contagious; in a few moments the walk was deserted.

Baker's strained voice reached them through the closed door, still calling angrily for help.

Gary grinned. He opened the door and stepped inside. Striking a match, he located the lamp on the sheriff's desk. The match went out before he reached it. He struck another, tilted the glass chimney and brought the flame to the wick.

A smoky orange-yellow light spread across the room. Baker quit yelling. Gary turned up the flame and watched the three gunmen file in. Doc walked behind them, heeled the door shut. He turned to the window and pulled down the shade, keeping his body out of line as he did so. Doc was a cautious man.

Across the room Judd Vestry slowly got up off the straw pallet where he had been lying. He came to the cell door, shaking his head. He watched Gary, his eyes glittering with implacable hate.

Gary took the keys from his pocket, walked to the cell which held Baker and opened it. The blocky man's jaw dropped when he saw whom he was having for company.

Sam Insted paused in the doorway, and Gary gave him a shove. The gunman stumbled forward.

61

He straightened and looked back, his eyes as muddy-colored as his face.

"I'll get out of here!" he whispered. "You'll never hold me. I'll get out, fella! An' when I do—"

"They'll bury you!" Gary said flatly.

The others sidled past him into the cell, and Gary slammed the door shut. Doc was across the room, standing by the front door. He was looking at Gary and through Gary—and the Kid sensed the coldness in the man, the barrier that had come up between them.

Judd's voice rasped in his ear. "How long do you intend to keep me here?"

Gary turned to him. "Until you get some sense in yore head," he snapped. He walked up to the old sheriff. "I didn't kill Bob. If you had any sense, you'd know—"

Judd spat at him. Gary's jaw knotted. "All right," he said bleakly. "Rot in there!" He turned and walked to the desk, his back stiff. He'd never convince this old man that he had not killed his son.

Doc's dry voice reached out to him. "You should have told us, Kid. Me and Jackson."

Gary looked at him. Doc's face was stony; it was a stranger's face.

Gary frowned. "I should have," he admitted. "But it wasn't an easy story to tell, Doc."

Doc's lips curled. "For five years I rode with a

kid I picked up on the trail. A button I found badly hurt—a boy with no home. Now I find he's a big shot—the boss of Big Hat." His voice held a curious hurt. "You should have told us, Kid!"

Gary's tone was impatient. "What does it matter who I am, Doc?"

"It does to me," Doc said bitterly. "Jackson fell into a trap—but I'm not going to be that much of a fool. We had a job, like a dozen others we've had, when we came here, Kid. Stop Yaegar and his bunch—for ten thousand dollars! That made sense to me. That's the way we worked." He shook his head. "Bucking Yaegar's guns so that you can take over the Big Hat—that doesn't sit well with me, Kid!"

Gary's voice was grim. "You'll still get your money, Doc!"

"Keep it!" Doc's voice was suddenly intense. "You've come a long way since Jackson and I picked you up. We taught you a lot—and you learned fast. You're hard and tough—and murder with that Colt. But tonight I saw a man beat you!" His smile was bitter. "You should have killed him when you had the chance, Kid."

"Jose?"

Doc nodded. "Just a reminder, when you buck Yaegar himself. Alone, Kid!"

"Where are *you* going?"

Doc paused at the door. "My business, Kid," he said softly.

Gary took a step toward him. "Doc, we can't break up now!"

Doc opened the door. "Can't we?" He closed it behind him. His boots scuffed softly on the walk, faded. . . .

Gary whirled at a thin snicker behind him. Judd was eyeing him, a sneer on his lips. The Kid blew out the light and walked out, locking the door behind him. He kept the keys with him. So far Baker's cries had brought no one willing to attempt a jail break. Either there were no other Yaegar men in town—or they were lying low.

But how long would it be before word got back to Yaegar himself that three—no, four—of his men were locked up? One of them his ace gunman, Sam Insted. How long before Yaegar rode into town to break them out?

He paused on the dark walk in front of the law office. Doc was gone. He felt the lack of the man's presence sharply. Doc had always been there, silent, dependable. They had worked as a team— he, Jackson and Doc. And now that team had fallen apart—

Where was Jackson? In Yaegar's place? He eyed the dark building across the square.

A man's voice rode the night air, loud and strangely clear. "All right, George. I'm ready to roll!"

Gary swung his attention to the stage, drawn up before the stage office a hundred yards away, on his side of Texas Square. Light spilled out into the street, outlining the coach, the restless horses.

The station man tossed his last sack up to the driver, who stowed it behind him. A whip cracked sharply in the night, followed by a high riding yell: "Aie-e-e-e!" The team lunged forward, kicking up dust that hung like a mist in the lamplight. The coach slewed around in a tight turn and went rolling toward Main Street, took a fast turn south and disappeared.

Gary's glance lingered at the corner. Ann was on that stage. Going where? He was still thinking of her when Ann said:

"I didn't go, Gary. . . ."

The Kid didn't move. He stood in the shadows, staring across the square. Finally he took in a deep breath, turned.

Ann came toward him, her heels making sharp clicking sounds on the boards. She came out of the splash of light, a tall, unsmiling girl, and into the shadows beside Gary.

"I'm staying in Del Rio," she said.

He faced her, feeling the wall of years between them. He had thought he knew this girl once—now it was like meeting a stranger. So he waited, not knowing what she wanted of him. . . .

She sensed his indrawn mood, and pride fought a brief battle in her. Her voice was strained, forced. "I'm sorry about this afternoon, Gary. I tried to hurt you, but I only hurt myself—"

He shrugged stiffly.

"I had decided to leave. I was going to Austin where I have an aunt—"

Gary's voice was brittle. "With your husband, Mrs. Sigleman?"

"My husband is dead!" He couldn't see her face clearly, but he sensed the strain in her. "He was killed a week after we were married, more than a year ago."

The wind came up from the south, bringing a strong whiff of fried onions. Texas Square lay deserted, brooding in the night. . . .

"I'm sorry, Ann," he said quietly.

She moved her shoulders. "I don't know if I loved him, Gary," she said in a small voice. "I didn't have a chance to find out." She let the silence run between them. Gary moved up to her. He put his hands on her shoulders and looked down into the dim whiteness of her face.

"I'm sorry he was killed," he said quietly.

She turned slightly, laying her glance against the darkened window of the law office. He sensed her question, and answered it. "Yes, he's still in there, Ann. I don't want to kill him!" His voice was suddenly thick in his throat. "I can't let him out!"

Ann nodded understandingly. "He's never been the same since Bob died, Gary. He didn't seem to care what happened to me, didn't bother with me. He was like a stranger—and I couldn't stand it. I was miserable and alone—and when Mort asked me—" She looked up into Gary's face. "He was the only man who was nice to me, who wanted me. You understand that, Gary?"

He nodded, feeling a sudden resentment for the bitter, stubborn lawman inside the law office. Judd Vestry and his father had had a lot in common, he reflected bitterly.

"But you're wrong about my father," Ann said softly. "He isn't a Yaegar man. He's neither for Yaegar nor for the Big Hat, Gary. Oh! I know it's wrong—I know how he would have been in the old days. Once, it would have been a three-cornered fight—with my father upholding the law between Yaegar and the Big Hat. Now—" She put a hand on his arm, her fingers tightening. "He'll hate me for telling you. But my father's crippled. He's not the Judd you knew. Six months after Bob died, he suffered a stroke. Only Doctor Morrison and I know that it has left his right side partially paralyzed. He's bluffed the Yaegar gunmen so far, Gary—they haven't dared push him into an open fight. But when they find out he's almost helpless—"

The Kid waited, letting her tell it in her own way; thinking that there was always something more to a man than appeared on the surface. Finally he said: "I didn't know, Ann."

She shivered a little. "I've seen it coming,

Gary—the showdown. Dad's avoided it, and they haven't pushed him so far. But it's coming. Tom Blake, your father's foreman, is getting desperate. He's told Dad either to back him—or be considered on Yaegar's side—"

"What about the feeling in town?" Gary interrupted.

"Del Rio's neutral," Ann replied. "So far it's been a range war—a fight between the Diamond Cross and the Big Hat. Yaegar's men haven't bothered anyone here—they've made no trouble. Some of the townsmen are even glad to get their business." Her tone lowered. "The Millers have never been too well liked in town."

Gary nodded. "Where are you staying, Ann?"

"At the hotel."

He took her arm. "I'll walk you there."

They went down the walk to the end of Texas Square and turned north on Main Street. The town seemed oddly quiet tonight. Most of the noise seemed to come from the Mexican section, from townsmen who didn't have a stake in the outcome of the fight between Yaegar and the Big Hat.

He paused by the hotel veranda, touched his hat. "Good night, Ann."

"Where will you stay, Gary?"

"I don't know." If he turned his head he could see the big house on the hill—the Castinado hacienda the Millers had taken over. But he didn't look. Somehow he didn't want to go back there. There were too many sour memories; too much had been left unsaid and undone there.

Ann's voice was soft. "I'm glad now that I didn't leave."

He watched her turn and go up the steps into the lobby. Then he swung away, walked back to Texas Square.

He paused on the corner and built himself a cigaret. Yaegar's loomed up, dark and challenging, across the wide, shadowed space. He thought of Doc and Jackson, and the plans they had made. What had gone wrong? Why had Doc been so touchy? Each man's past was his own—it had been an unspoken agreement between them. Why had Doc walked out now? Because of the guns behind Yaegar?

He found no answer that fitted.

Restless and impatient, he walked back toward the law office. A wedge of light from a saloon at his elbow fell across several horses nudging the rail. One of them was Jackson's big gray!

Gary stopped. Jackson was a strange man, a brooding man. Had he turned in here and forgotten the meeting at Pedro's? He could have. For Jackson, as Gary well knew, had his own devils riding him.

The Kid turned and shoved his way through the cantina doors.

A smoky light from two overhead lamps showed him only a scattering of customers in the room.

Some were playing cards—two were footing the brass rail.

The bartender, a one-armed man with a shapeless, unshaven face, was dozing. He opened one eye as Gary came in, and his whole body came alert, like a cat waking.

Gary walked to the bar. Jackson was not in sight.

"I'm looking for a big man," he said levelly. He ignored the bartender's seeming fascination with the badge on his shirt. "Red hair—a scar over his left eye."

The one-armed man licked his lips. "A beeg man, *señor*?"

One of the rail drinkers turned his head, showing a sudden interest. "Sure," he growled. "Sure—he was in here." His glance went to Gary's badge. "You a new one—Deppity?"

Gary said levelly: "I'm looking for Jackson."

The other grinned sourly. He had on old range clothes. Rope burns had left their whitish scars on his gnarled hands. Not a young man, and out of a job. He gave that impression to Gary Miller.

"Thought you'd know," he said. Gary frowned at the defiance in the man's tone. "If you're a Yaegar man—"

"I ain't!" Gary snapped.

The ex-puncher absorbed this. He had been drinking; it showed in the high flush on his horsy face. It probably explained the reckless glint in his eyes.

70

"Jackson's dead!" He saw Gary stiffen, and his lips turned down harshly. "I was here when he walked in. A big fella with red hair and a scar over his eye. He asked about Red Becker!" The puncher laughed harshly. "That's a dirty name around here—less'n yo're a Yaegar man. No one answered him right off. Then Slim started to tell him—and he was killed before he could get it out—"

"Slim?"

"Yeah. Slim used to ride for the Big Hat, like me." The man stepped away from the bar, showing Gary a stiffened left leg. "I got this working for the Big Hat, Deppity."

Gary's lips tightened. "What about Jackson?"

"Sure—sure." The puncher jerked a thumb to the door. "The sheriff came in after Slim was shot. He didn't care about Slim. Didn't seem to care about Jackson. Didn't even ask the big fella why he wanted Becker. He said Becker had just come to town and was in Yaegar's—across the square."

The horse-faced man shrugged. "We watched the big fella head across the square, into Yaegar's. We heard two shots. He didn't come out!"

Gary felt tiredness seep through him, numbing him. He turned and caught the bartender's eye. "Where's Slim's body?"

"In back." The one-armed man's voice was neutral. "I send a man for Tom Blake, Big Hat foreman. Told him to come get the body."

Gary turned to the lamed puncher. "You said you worked for the Big Hat," he observed levelly. "You quit?"

The other nodded.

"You're hired, if you want to come back," Gary said.

The puncher scowled. "Hired? Who's hirin' me?"

"I am!" Gary walked up to him. "I'm Gary Miller."

The puncher hesitated, not believing him. Gary added flatly: "It's been six years since the last time I went up to the Big Hat. I don't know how many of the old hands are left. But if Tom Blake comes to town tonight, he'll know me. Blake's been with the Big Hat since I got out of the crawling stage."

"Gary Miller!" The puncher's tone held a question. "I've heard of you. Heard Tom Blake say you'd been run out of town." He hesitated, making up his mind. Then he turned, reached across the bar for a clean glass. He pushed the glass and his bottle in front of Gary.

"Name's Larry Main. If you're Gary Miller, Tom Blake's been waiting for you a heck of a long time. . . ."

Shadows shrouded the trail to El Paso. Patches of cloud obscured the low-hanging stars. The moon was a faint sliver in the sky and cast little light.

Doc rode without haste. The shadowy forms of the Kid and Jackson rode with him, nagging him. Their presence was there beside him—he couldn't shake the feeling.

The Kid should have told us, he argued silently. But he knew it was something deeper than the Kid's close-mouthedness that had hurt him.

The moon went down and an early morning chill crept over the land. The road crested a long bare ridge and went down in loops to the flat stretch of land lost in the darkness.

Doc reined in, finally facing a bitter fact, admitting it to himself. He and Jackson had picked up the Kid, a wounded lost youngster who had never once mentioned home or talked of his parents. A tight-mouthed boy who had grown up under his tutelage and had seemed content.

He had always looked upon the Kid that way— as someone who needed him. He hadn't realized his own need—had not realized how much the Kid had come to take the place of the son he had lost at birth to a woman he had never forgiven.

He brought the palm of his hand over his face and shut his tired eyes. Ahead lay the trail to El Paso, to longer years of drifting.

Behind him was a youngster who needed him, and a redheaded giant who was already in trouble.

Behind him lay Yaegar's guns. . . .

He took a deep breath. The dismal foreboding with which he had viewed Del Rio from the rimrock yesterday morning oppressed him again. He had been a fatalist all his life, and the feeling was strong in him at this moment that if he turned back now he'd never leave Del Rio.

The animal under him snorted tiredly, rousing him to its need. He turned off the trail and rode a short way across a sandy wash, pale under the stars. A live-oak grew at the edge of the wash, casting its thick pattern of shadow. Doc dismounted, turned his cayuse loose on a picket rope, and spread his blankets. But he was too troubled to sleep.

He sat with his back against the tree, smoking, looking into the night. . . .

CHAPTER VIII

Pedro closed early. It was the first time since he had opened the Café Reale, nearly thirty years ago, that he had closed before two in the morning. He was closed by ten-thirty.

He drew the narrow shades down over the glass panels in the double doors which backed up the swinging ones and walked back across the sawdust-sprinkled floor. He was a heavy man and his tread was heavy.

He stood by the deserted bar and looked down where blood darkened and stained several spots on the floor. Spilled blood was not new to the Café Reale. But the violence which had gathered to a head here still lingered. Pedro shuddered. He was not a coward, but the thin-lipped viciousness of the men who had broken loose here was beyond him. These were moods he couldn't quite under-stand.

A man raised a fist or pulled a knife, or, if he was good enough, pulled a gun in a savage fit of anger. This he understood. To come in seeking to kill in cold and calculated fashion—he shook his head and uncorked a bottle still setting on the counter and drank from it.

Normally Pedro was not a whiskey drinker. Whiskey was for the *Anglos*, the tall, thin-lipped breed who liked their liquor raw and burning. Pedro preferred his *cerveza*, a Mexican beer, or a red table wine. . . . But this was a time for whiskey.

He felt the raw liquor belt him with fiery impact, and he brushed his thick lips with the back of his hairy arm. It was quiet upstairs, but then, listening, he heard Carmelita's voice, soft and throaty, singing: *"Pero ando ingrato si con mi amor no quedo. . . ."*

El Abandonado . . . Carmelita's favorite song.

A peasant girl, wild as the hills from which she came . . . she carried a torch for Jose. Perhaps, he thought, she was happier now with her man wounded than if he had killed Gary Miller.

Remembering the Miller boy who had come back made Pedro anxious again. He had to get Jose out of here. He had a dead man lying in his back room now, one of Yaegar's men, killed by that Mexican upstairs. And while his sympathies lay with the swaggering, dark-eyed Mexican, he knew his existence depended on not showing any favoritism.

If Jose remained here, Yaegar would tear the café apart to get him!

He corked the bottle and put it away on his back shelf and washed the dirty glasses which remained. Pedro was a methodical man. Then he took off his apron and hung it on a nail and went upstairs.

Carmelita had been living in one of his upstairs rooms since he had hired her to sing and entertain his customers. He had found her dark beauty attracted both breeds which inhabited Del Rio, and although she often was the center of fights, he figured she brought him more than enough business to compensate for the little he paid her.

That was until Jose started getting possessive . . . and when Jose got possessive he had put a wall around her; a wall few men dared to scale.

Now Pedro would be glad to get rid of her.

He could hear her more clearly now as he rounded the stairs into the hallway. She was crooning softly, like a mother to her child—and Pedro smiled at the thought. To Carmelita, Jose probably was all things—a child, too, at this moment, in need of her.

He knocked on the door and then, when he was disregarded, he knocked louder. Carmelita's sharp voice questioned: "Who is it?"

"Me. Pedro."

"Go away." Her voice was softer, but there was a fierce possessiveness in it. "He is sleeping. . . ."

Pedro opened the door and went in. He stood by the bed where Carmelita sat with Jose's head pillowed in her lap. A basin with blood-dyed water stood on a chair close by. . . . He saw that Jose's arm was well bandaged.

Jose's gun arm! The slim Mexican would never get over it. His arrogance had stemmed from his ability with that weapon at his hip. . . . He had walked tall among these cold-eyed *Anglos* because of it. Now he would be forever a slinking coyote. . . .

"You must leave here," he said. "Immediately."

Carmelita's eyes flashed. "You are crazy, Pedro! He is hurt. That gringo's bullet smashed bone—*muy diablo*!" Tears wet her eyes, making the anger in them brighter. "Jose will never use his arm again, Pedro!"

Pedro nodded. "I know. That is more reason why you should leave now, before Yaegar comes to town."

Carmelita's hand slipped down her leg, and a knife glittered in the lamplight. "No one will harm Jose—"

"He would kill you with no more thought than he would give to the killing of Jose," Pedro said. His voice was rougher now, his patience strained. "You must get him out of here tonight."

"How? Where?"

"By chance yore father is in town," he said. "He is in Antonio's. . . ." Pedro lifted mountainous shoulders. "You know yore father, Carmelita. He should be happy by this hour . . . happy with Antonio's mescal in him. In another hour he will even forgive you. . . ."

"No." Carmelita's eyes held a dark stubbornness. "I swore by the Holy Mother I would never go back!"

"Where else can you take him?" Pedro snapped. "You want him to die? And he will surely die when Yaegar comes!"

Carmelita's defiance faded. "He is still there, my father?"

"*Si.*" Pedro turned as he heard the downstairs back door close. It was a soft sound, but he had an ear cocked for sounds tonight. "I sent Tomas to make sure. Yore father's cart is in Antonio's yard. I will have Tomas help you. Put Jose in the cart; cover him with straw. Perhaps you should lie with him. . . . Yaegar would be immediately suspicious, if he ran into you riding on the seat with yore father."

Carmelita nodded. "You are right, Pedro—it is the only way. And I will stay with him until he is well again. And then, perhaps, we will leave here . . . go to Mexico. I want him to forget this land that once belonged to his ancestors."

Pedro nodded, but he had his doubts. Jose would never forget. He had grown up remembering. . . .

Tomas knocked discreetly, and he growled, "Come in." The swamper and general handyman shuffled inside, hat in hand. . . . He was broad of face and shoulder and thick between the ears. He had the placid good humor of an ox.

"*Si*—Felippe ees still in Antonio's. He ees singin', *Señor* Pedro . . . singin' of the lost sheep in the hills. . . ."

"Let him sing," Pedro said. He pointed to Jose.

"I want you to carry him to Felippe's cart. Lay him inside, gently, and then return here. I will have a bottle for Felippe—so that he may sing more. . . ."

Tomas nodded. He walked to the bed and slid his arm under Jose and lifted the man as though he were a baby. Jose groaned. But the liquor and the shock of his wound combined to put him in a dull stupor. . . . He lay limp across Tomas's shoulder as the man turned away.

Carmelita remained behind just long enough to scoop up her few personal belongings into a small bag. Then she followed Tomas.

Pedro waited by the bar. Ten minutes later Tomas returned. He handed the man the bottle of tequila for Felippe. Tomas smiled. "He will come more willingly, *señor*, when he sees this. He was not pleased to see his daughter. . . . Ah, it is a shame, no. But he does not know of Jose. I put him in the cart, as you said. . . . Carmelita went to see him. He would not even look at her. But she will be in the cart when Felippe leaves—and he will not know, and in a little while he will not even care. . . ."

Pedro shrugged. "It is Felippe's affair, not mine." He prepared to blow out the lights.

Tomas turned. "That gringo who shot Jose . . . he and some rider from the Beeg Hat. They have just gone into Yaegar's, Pedro!"

Pedro stiffened. He waved Tomas away, but he

remained in the empty room, listening. He waited a long while, but he heard no sounds of gunfire, which puzzled him.

After that he blew out the lights and went upstairs. He lay awake a long time, still listening. . . . His sleep, when it came, was troubled.

Larry Main let his unlighted cigaret droop limply from the corner of his mouth. The night was warm, but not warm enough to account for the tiny beads of sweat on his forehead.

"You hired me," he said. "I'm going in there with you, Gary."

Gary Miller stood in the shadows on the walk outside the saloon doors, out of the light which spilled under and over the slatted doors and showed him Jackson's big gray. The animal recognized him and whinnied hungrily . . . it had been a long day.

The old Palacio Verde, now Yaegar's, loomed across the square, dark-windowed and waiting. If Jackson went in there after Becker he was probably already dead; from what Larry Main had told him Jackson had been lured into a trap. But the man had come to Del Rio with the Kid, in good faith, and though it was his own private business which had taken him into Yaegar's, Gary felt a grim responsibility for his partner.

Doc's words still stung. He could understand Doc's anger. But the man had given him little chance to explain his paramount reasons for coming back . . . and he couldn't have put into words his feelings about Ann or the nagging desire to return and clear himself with Ann and Judd Vestry whom he had once idolized.

Unconsciously his hand came up to brush the badge he had pinned on his shirt. Ann had cleared up some things about Judd, but Ann would never convince the old lawman that he had not killed Bob Vestry that night, long ago, when he, Bob and Jose had planned to run away from home.

He heard Larry fidget, and his thoughts came back to the dark building across the street, and he knew he had to find out what had happened to Jackson.

"Cover me," he said, and stepped to the restless gray tied at the rack and slid Jackson's heavy Sharps from the scabbard. He handed it to the puncher, who grinned. "I'm better with a rifle any day. . . ."

But Gary was already off the walk, moving across the street, a lean, wide-shouldered youngster with the prowling motion of a big cat. He was across the road and into the shadows. There was no movement from Yaegar's, and a hunch came to Gary.

Jackson was not in Yaegar's, nor was anyone else. Not anyone of consequence.

He came up to the door and tried it and was

not unduly surprised to find it unlocked. . . . He swung it open and stood in the shadows, peering at an angle into the big room which had been old Miguel Aragon's pride and joy.

The room was dark and the big crystal chandeliers imported from Mexico City caught some stray gleam and glittered faintly. . . . He smelled the reek of stale tobacco and sour beer, and with it the clinging odor of sweat from long unwashed bodies.

The Palacio Verde had been class when Gary was a boy. . . . Yaegar had turned it into an ordinary saloon.

He heard Larry limp across the street and clump up the stairs and join him in the shadows. The man's breathing came a bit fast. "Nobody in?"

Gary shrugged. "Let's take a look—"

He twisted around the door framing and was in darkness again, away from the faint outline of the door. He knew this big room well enough; he didn't need light to find the stairs.

He heard Larry's quick breathing behind him, and he sensed the loyalty in this man who was not a gunfighter by choice or inclination and yet was following him into what might well be a gun trap.

He tried the door at the foot of the stairs and found it locked. It opened to what had been Miguel's office. Gary could only guess that it was still used for the same purpose.

His hunch grew stronger, but he kept his caution in hand. . . . He went quickly up the stairs to the big balcony and the small private rooms which opened on it. These had once been private gaming rooms.

He found an old, dried-up man in one. He stirred in the darkness, and his stirring creaked bed springs. . . . Gary thumbed a match to flame in his left hand while his right muzzled a Colt toward the bed.

In the small, flickering glow he saw the man—pock-faced, shaggy-haired. The reek of whiskey lay thick in this room.

Yaegar's swamper, he thought bleakly. Left alone, he had probably helped himself to bar stock and then crawled up here to sleep it off. Gary's eyes narrowed as the flame burned down; he let the match drop and put his heel on it.

"Just the bum Yaegar keeps around to sweep up," Larry breathed. "Looks like they've all gone."

"Except Sam Insted and a couple of others," Gary said. "Reckon Yaegar, or whoever was in here tonight, thought that would be enough to take care of things in town. I don't reckon any of them will be back before tomorrow."

Larry turned to him in the dark; Gary could feel the probe of the man's eyes. "Sam Insted? Where is he?"

"In jail," Gary said shortly, and turned away.

The swamper turned over and began to snore heavily. . . .

They went back down the stairs and out onto the walk. Gary paused. A two-wheeled cart rumbled by, pulled by an ox. The man in the seat was small, wiry, dried-up and brown as the country. . . . He was singing off-key but in a liquor-pleasant voice. An old Mexican ballad of the days of Cortez. . . .

"Old Felippe, the goat herder," Larry said, and there was a cowman's sneer in his identification. But Gary had recognized the man without Larry's comment—he had known Felippe from the days of his boyhood, when they had played around the goat camp.

"He came here," Larry said, puzzled. He was talking of Jackson, Gary knew. "I saw him—" He shrugged. "We all heard a shot . . . but he was nobody we knew, and the sheriff didn't give a hoot. He stood right there on the walk in front of the saloon and just smiled that hard smile he has. . . . Then he turned and walked away."

Jackson was dead, Gary thought. They might have left his body here for him to find. Or Red Becker might have taken Jackson's body to Yaegar—to the Diamond Cross. Either way, there was little he could do for the big fellow now, except avenge him, when the showdown came.

It would come soon enough, he thought coldly. Yaegar would not take what had happened here tonight without hitting back. And he knew he could not stand up to Yaegar alone—not against Yaegar and the guns that would be with Yaegar.

Doc was gone—and so was Jackson. And the wry thought occurred to him that maybe Doc was right. Even drunk, Jose Castinado had shaded him. . . . And Yaegar was faster than Jose!

He turned to Larry Main. "Ride the big fellow's gray," he said. "We're heading for Big Hat."

Larry grinned. "Tom Blake'll be glad to see you, Gary!"

CHAPTER IX

They rode out of Del Rio, taking the trail under the hill on which the Miller house stood limned against the stars. It was the old Castinado house, hardly changed when his father, Dwayne Miller, had taken over . . . it was a place he remembered with little love.

He had liked the sprawling ranchhouse at the Big Hat better. . . . There was neither pretense there, nor a grandeur inappropriate to the Millers. So he glanced up at the house where a wide window held the yellow glow of lamplight. He thought of his Uncle Henry, and he was content to let the man dwell in his fancied glory in the big house.

He rode past the hill and out onto the widening run of the valley. . . . Larry looked back once and said tonelessly: "Big house, Gary, for just one man. . . ."

Gary Miller made no answer to this. They rode at a lope which soon caused them to catch up with Felippe, and swung around him in a silent detour. The man had fallen asleep, his head on his chest. The ox plodded on. . . . It knew the road as well as the man on the cart. Six miles farther on it would take the rutted road that forked to the left, and another seven miles would bring him to Felippe's mud hut. . . .

They rode past, and Gary glanced at the cart and noticed that the high-sided wagon bed seemed filled with loose straw. He had a moment's brief wonder as to what Felippe wanted with this, and then he forgot it.

The stars wheeled in the sky, and Gary knew it was past midnight when they came down the long slope and saw the pattern of Big Hat before them.

Poplars shaded the road to the sprawling ranch-house, and several big pepper trees, reaching out like dark umbrellas, cast their shadows over the corrals and outbuildings.

The river flowed unhurriedly between low banks less than a quarter of a mile away. . . . Not until it hit the barrier of the Blackrocks and plunged through Blackrock Canyon would the placid stream change, swiften, become a narrow spillway at the Rio Grande.

Gary loved the ranch. . . . He reined in now and looked down at the only pleasant memories of his boyhood.

Beyond the river the Blackrocks lay lost in the night. In those hills Yaegar waited for the time when he'd come down and take Big Hat. . . . Gary's horse snorted heavily in the darkness.

He looked at Larry, waiting silently. "Let's wake up Tom Blake," he said quietly. "I've got a lot of talking to do. . . ."

Far behind, Felippe's oxcart rumbled through the night. The ox took the fork and leaned into his collar. . . . The narrow road went up into the bare hills, looping along their slopes like a loose brown ribbon. The stars began to pale in the sky and the ox snorted heavily, a yellow-brown froth lacing his wide nostrils. But this was not the first time he had come home from Del Rio in the night.

The cart creaked on its wooden axle and the weight in it shifted. Carmelita thrust her head above the loose straw and looked up at the sky. She felt safe now from stray riders. . . . Jose was moaning softly. She felt his pain as though it were her own. . . . She threw out the straw which covered them and bent over him and kissed him lightly.

He stirred and his eyes opened . . . they were black and without expression. Then pain stirred in them and he said hoarsely: "Where are we, Carmelita?"

"On the way home," she said. "Where I was born."

He digested this slowly through his pain-fogged mind. He shook his head. "No!" He tried to raise himself, his eyes bitter. "I won't stay in a stinking goat herd's hut, Carmelita. Not me, Jose Castinado!"

Felippe roused on the seat. He ran his fingers across his face and stared stupidly at the lightening sky. . . . The ox was quickening its pace now as he headed down into the small bowl-like clearing under a rock-studded hill. The mud and rock shack with its adobe-walled corral was a dark splotch in the distance.

Jose stood up. He swayed and fell against the high board side and nearly pitched out, and Carmelita held him. Felippe turned in his seat. "*Quien es?*" His voice was thick.

Below them a dog barked a welcome, and after a moment a light came on in the one window facing them. A billygoat baaahed his greeting, and it was taken up by others in the corral. . . . The dog barked louder, running back and forth in the yard.

Jose's eyes held a dark bitterness. "Felippe the goat herd's place! This is where you brought me?"

The girl's voice was contrite. "Only until you get well, Jose. Then we will leave. We'll go to Mexico. I will find a job in a *cantina*. . . . I weel sing. For you, Jose. . . ."

He shoved her away from him. "You little fool! You think I would go away while the man who did this to me lives?"

"What can you do now?" she questioned hesitantly, and shrank away from the fury in his eyes.

"I have another arm!" he snarled. "A hand that can hold a gun. That will be enough, Carmelita. Enough to kill Gary Meeler. . . ."

"You forget," she whispered, "the talk you made tonight. Talk which already is being whispered in the ears of Yaegar." She came close to him while the wagon jolted in the ruts and Felippe muttered in drunken stupor. "They'll kill you on sight now—kill you as they would a snake they find on the trail!"

The wagon was coming into the yard now, and the dog, a shaggy shepherd, came barking around the ox. A woman was waiting in the door of the hut, the lamplight dim behind her. A dumpy, short woman with stolid features that showed her Indian blood. Behind her, peering over her shoulder, was the narrow bright-eyed face of one of Carmelita's four brothers.

Carmelita jumped out of the cart. She ran to the woman who had borne her, her orders crisp. "*Mi hombre*," she said. "He is hurt. He will stay here with us until he is well!"

Her mother said nothing. She made no move to help her. Carmelita stared at her, anger rising in a dark flood. . . . She tossed her head and went back to the cart where Jose was trying to climb over the side.

He slipped and fell as she reached him, and they went down together. He banged his arm against the high wheel and groaned once, his face paling with the brutal stab of pain. His slim body went limp.

Carmelita turned to the door. "Americo!" she called her brother. "Help me with Jose!"

The boy came out slowly into the yard. The dog was still barking, mingling his excited greeting with the baaahing of the goats. The eastern sky was paling fast now, drawing its veil of light over the stars.

He turned to look at his mother, and found no answer to his mute question. Carmelita was trying to drag Jose to the shack. Americo went to her and gave her a hand.

Felippe had stepped down from the seat. He stood staring in that dull, sightless way while the ox waited patiently to be unyoked and led to the small shed and fed.

Carmelita and her brother dragged Jose to the door. Her mother stood in their way, a stolid, immovable bulk. "Help him!" Carmelita said, and there was no sharpness in her voice, no anger now. "Help him, *mia madre!*"

The woman moved aside. She went to Felippe, who was standing by the wheel, and took him by the hand and led him back to the house. This she did every time Felippe went to Del Rio . . . a matter of once a month. Then she went out and took care of the ox.

And finally she came back and looked down at Jose's pinched white face. She uttered one guttural sound, an affirmative, and turned into the hut.

Between them Carmelita and Americo lifted Jose and carried him inside. . . .

Red Becker slid the point of his pocket knife under Jackson's fingernail and watched the big man jerk in the chair. Red watched his eyes roll and open and saw the pain in them, and laughed with cruel abandon.

Two other men, thin-lipped, wiry, were in the Diamond Cross bunkhouse. They were playing cards, but their game was desultory and one of them looked a little sick. After a while he threw his cards on the table and stalked out.

Becker paid little attention to them. He was a tall man who had gone to flesh; his shoulders were heavy and his stomach bulged over his belt. The ruddy goods looks of his younger years had changed subtly; at first glance there was still the impression of handsome features, until a closeup revealed the puffiness and the swollen capillaries and a general seaminess.

He stood over Jackson, one boot planted on the seat of a chair, looking down on this big man who had hounded him through the years, until at last he had fled into Mexico where he had joined Yaegar.

He had known Jackson would be in Del Rio, and the trap had been set. . . . They had taken the big man without killing him. A clubbed Colt from behind, while Jackson's shot went wild, tearing upward, into the ceiling at Yaegar's.

It had not been Becker's idea, this taking Jackson alive. He had wanted to kill Jackson. But Yaegar was the boss, and no man crossed Yaegar. Take him to the Diamond Cross, Yaegar had ordered, alive.

Becker had complied. Yaegar was not at the hole-in-the-hills ranch when he got here with Jackson—Becker had not expected him to be. Yaegar had his own mysterious rendezvous, and no one questioned him.

They bound Jackson securely to the chair in the bunkhouse, and Becker proceeded with cold fury to give the helpless man a beating. And when Jackson slipped into unconsciousness, he had brought the man back with the pen knife trick. . . .

He could see the cold and savage fury in Jackson's eyes, glazed over with pain. The big man lunged against the rope holding him, his shoulders knotting; the sturdy chair creaked.

Becker backhanded Jackson across his bloody face. He was lifting his hand again when a thin-pitched voice snarled: "That's enough, Red! I've had all I kin stomach. Kill him if you want! But no more of that!"

Becker turned, his eyes glinting. The slim rider who had remained at the card table was on his feet now, his palm on the butt of his Colt. He was twenty, not more, and the splash of freckles across his nose stood out sharply.

"I'll kill him when I'm ready, Eddie! When I've had my fun with him!"

"Not here! Not any more!" Eddie's voice shook, but he was not afraid of Becker. "You'll leave him alone tonight!"

Becker took a slow breath. The other rider appeared in the bunkhouse doorway; he stood there, watching, his eyes bright and his face a muddy color. He looked as if he might have been sick.

Becker considered the situation. If he persisted he'd have to kill Eddie, and maybe Eddie's brother, Nat. And Yaegar wouldn't like it. . . .

He turned away from Jackson, walked toward the far bunk. He shucked his boots and his hat and took off his gun rig. This he hung on the nail close by, where he could reach it in a hurry.

He lay on the bunk then, his hands behind his head . . . lay there waiting. Jackson's tortured breathing was a heavy sound in the bunkhouse. Nat came into the bunkhouse and slid into the chair across from his brother. Eddie picked up the cards and began to shuffle. . . .

Others began drifting into the bunkhouse. A motley crew, held together in a loose alliance. Most of them were Border scum. They rode for Yaegar and they took his orders, and only money held them together. They were a clanny crew—

most of them were paired off—like the Maynerd brothers, Eddie and Nat.

They drifted in and waited, eyeing Jackson's slumped figure with only casual interest. Jackson was Becker's special interest—the big man did not concern them.

It was close to midnight when Yaegar came to the Diamond Cross. He turned his big black stallion over to one of the men smoking by the corral and went into the bunkhouse.

Becker sat up when Yaegar entered. The others straightened out of unconscious deference to this man. . . . The Maynerd brothers ceased playing cards.

He stood in the doorway, eyeing them all; his glance held on the back of the big man slumped in the chair.

Yaegar! That was the only name these men knew him by. A tall, hawk-faced man in his forties—a lean and rangy man with the calm, disciplined face of a judge and hair not yet beginning to gray. He wore black broadcloth, like some itinerant preacher—but few preachers wore crossing gun belts, or could use heavy Frontier Colts like those in his oiled holsters with such efficiency.

Yaegar—born John Ellis Cunningham—had once been privately tutored. Later he had studied law, given that up to study medicine. He had found neither pursuit satisfying to his restless nature and had turned to gambling. A series of bad nights with the cards and he was heavily in debt. A man's sneering remarks at a fashionable bar, concerning worthless I.O.U.'s, had led to an early morning duel. He had left the man dying on the dew-fresh grass and had fled the state . . . had headed West, beyond the Mississippi, as others had done before him.

In time John Cunningham had become Yaegar—gambler, gunman, gun-boss. He was in Mexico, in a small dusty town across the border, when a proposition was put to him. He had accepted.

Standing there, looking at Jackson's broad back, he knew that the plans which had been outlined in that dusty Mexican town were coming to a head. . . . His smile was tempered as he walked into the narrow room to stand over the bound man.

He studied Jackson's swollen, bloody face; then his glance went to Becker, sitting on his bunk. Becker's eyes met his with sullen defiance.

"You should have been an Apache," Yaegar said. There was an edge of contempt in his voice. "I wonder what you'd do if I untied him."

Becker's eyes narrowed. "I'd kill him," he said coldly.

Yaegar shrugged. "I reckon you would, the slow way. . . ." He stooped and put his forefinger under Jackson's chin and lifted the man's head and stared bleakly into Jackson's burning gaze.

He let Jackson's head drop and turned to Becker, and his voice was softer, and more dangerous because of it.

"I want him alive, Red—for the time being. And the next time you lay a finger on him, you'll answer to me for it!"

Becker stiffened. "I'll leave him alone," he muttered finally. "But I'll do the killin', when the time comes!"

Yaegar ignored him. A rider had come into the dark yard, wheeling his mount to a stop by the door. He dismounted and came into the bunkhouse . . . a small, weasel-faced man in town clothes. He was a hanger-on in Del Rio, a man who sometimes worked in Zeke's Livery. His name was Tootle.

Yaegar turned to face him, and the man froze just inside the door. . . . Behind him loomed one of Yaegar's riders, a tall hombre known as Luke. The gun he held against the newcomer's back brought sweat to the small man's face.

"Thought you oughta know, Yaegar!" he blurted out. "Know what happened in town—" He hunched his thin shoulders and cast a frightened look over his shoulder.

"Let him be, Luke!" Yaegar said.

The tall rider pouched his gun and stepped back, leaning against the door frame.

Tootle licked his lips. "Oughta be worth something," he began. His eyes shuttled over the cold-faced men. "Oughta be worth fifty bucks . . . mebbe. . . ."

"What happened in town?" Yaegar's tone had a steel edge which made the small man flinch.

"I was in Pedro's when it happened," Tootle said hurriedly. "Saw it all—" His Adam's apple bobbed in his scrawny throat. "Was there when Slim walked in an' had words with Jose. Jose killed him."

He saw Yaegar's eyes flame and he felt the sharp attention of the others, and his sense of importance came back and gave him a touch of confidence. "Heard Jose tell Slim to go to blazes. And he said the same for you, Yaegar."

Luke came away from the frame and shoved him. Tootle stumbled in the room, and Yaegar, stepping toward him like a prowling tiger, caught him. He jerked the small man up so that only his toes touched the floor. . . . His eyes held a murderous glint.

"Is that what you came to tell me?"

Tootle gasped. "Only the beginnin'—" He took a shaky breath as Yaegar let him down. "Sam Insted's in jail with Keene an' Grogan. An' Jose's shot up. Don't know how bad—"

The words came in a rush; he paused to catch his breath. "That's what I came to tell you!" he mumbled.

"Sam in jail?" Yaegar's eyes held a narrowing anger. This was not part of the pattern. He had left a gun trap in Del Rio that should have functioned smoothly. Sam Insted, Slim Trevor and Red Becker—with Keene and Grogan. He had never fully counted on Jose Castinado. . . .

"I handled my job," Becker said harshly. "Sam was waiting in yore office . . . he slugged Jackson. I packed him out here. Luke rode out with me. Sam figgered he and Slim could handle the Kid and Doc. Keene and Grogan were gonna hang around to see the fun. . . ."

"Ain't all that young feller did," Tootle put in, his voice thin. "Heard him called Gary Miller. He's got Baker in jail, too. An' Judd Vestry—"

Yaegar smiled bleakly.

Tootle hesitated. He had borrowed a horse from Zeke's Livery without Zeke's consent; he had come on an impulse, an impulse compounded of greed and a desire to ingratiate himself with Yaegar. Now he licked his lips, his pale eyes searching the hawk-nosed man's face. The grim silence of the men in the bunkhouse made him uneasy.

"I thought you'd like to know," he said. His voice was just above a squeaky whisper.

Yaegar nodded. "It's worth fifty dollars, Tootle." He gestured toward the near bunk. "You can use Slim Trevor's bunk tonight. You can ride back with us in the morning."

The gun boss's gaze reached out to every man in the bunkhouse. It came to Jackson, who had

obviously heard everything Tootle said. Something in the stiff line of the big man's back
annoyed him.

"Red—you stay here. Luke, too. Keep an eye on
him—" He gestured to Jackson. "The rest of you
will ride with me. We're going into Del Rio and
rip that jail apart . . . and we'll teach that tough
Kid a lesson. One he'll never benefit from—
because he'll be dead!"

He turned then, and walked out. . . .

CHAPTER X

Doc came into Del Rio with the sun at his back. His mounted shadow rode ahead of him, long and thin in the early morning. . . . He rode slack in the saddle and his face was grave.

He had spent most of the warm night smoking, looking into the dark corners of his life. Trying to find what had driven him these years. Trying to justify himself for walking out on the Kid.

He had dozed finally and awakened with dawn graying the sky. . . . There was a chill in his bones that reached into his soul.

Del Rio! He was a fatalist, Doc was—and he knew that his destiny was in this town. The end of a long and sometimes wearying trail—and he rode to meet it without regret.

He came into Del Rio from the river side and crossed over, splashing in the shallows. . . . He came up to the street that led into Texas Square, with a dog sniffing at his cayuse's heels.

The sun was barely warm against his back. Doc knuckled the gray-shot bristle along his jaw. He came in through the Mexican quarter of town, and he heard the early cries of little children, and the smells of breakfast tainted the air. It was, he thought with weary cynicism, the recurring cycle of the day; the dull routine of living.

A man slept and wakened, and ate his three meals and slept again. . . . In between a man worked or fought, loved or hated, and counted the day good or bad according to his own lights.

Silently, he rode into the sun-beaten amphitheater of Texas Square.

Yaegar's loomed up on his right, quiet and drowsing in the morning light. Across the street from the old Aragon place, in front of the saloon where Jackson's gray had been tethered last night, a one-eyed man came out to the plank walk and slopped dirty water from a bucket into the street. He straightened up and eyed Doc with studied interest; then he turned and shouldered through the batwings.

Doc wondered if the Kid had spent the night in Del Rio, and what had become of Jackson's gray.

He turned and glanced back at Yaegar's Saloon, appraising the windows fronting the square. Narrow windows, set deep inside thick adobe walls. A man could look down into the old plaza from any one of those apertures and not be seen from the street.

The sheriff's office looked dingy in the harsh morning light. A long, narrow building with a flat roof, it ran back into a small, littered yard. On an impulse Doc turned his animal to the empty rack.

The door was locked. He peered in through the window and saw no one in the office, but one of the men in the cells started yelling.

Doc hesitated. He went back to his horse and took a small probe from his black bag, and with it he picked the simple lock. He walked into the office and looked at the men still in the cells.

The man who had been yelling fell silent, scowling at him. Sam Insted sneered and turned away from the bars. Judd Vestry was sitting on his cot, shoulders slumped. He lifted his head from his hands and appraised Doc.

Doc ignored the Yaegar men. He walked up to the sheriff's cell, and his voice was gentle. "Where's the Kid, Judd?"

Vestry looked at him with remote interest; Doc meant nothing to him. He made no answer to Doc's question, but he asked one of his own, remembering last night. "You and the Kid had a falling out?"

Doc shrugged. "A mistake," he said coldly. "Mine."

Judd settled back on the cot and the hope went out of his eyes. Doc walked back to the desk and rummaged around. He found a deputy's badge in a drawer and toyed with it.

The law was not a matter of a brightly-shaped nickel badge. Nor was it a matter of the wearer's personal whims. The law in Del Rio had abdicated to an old man's desire for vengeance—and the law was now a matter of the fastest gun.

Doe's fingers closed tightly over the badge, and

the smile on his lips was thin and mocking. Slowly he pinned the badge to his coat.

Behind him Sam Insted sneered: "That tin badge ain't gonna help you, Doc, when Yaegar comes to town!"

"Maybe you're right," Doc said, not turning. "But life is full of surprises, Sam. . . ."

He walked to the door and stood on the threshold, a sombre man with no immediate purpose in mind. If the Kid was in Del Rio he'd see him soon enough; if Gary had left town there was little he could do but wait. He stood in the doorway, and his attention was caught by the bright-wheeled gig that came into the square, pulled by a high-stepping thoroughbred gelding.

It swung around the old fountain in the middle of the plaza and came to the sheriff's office, pulling up by the hitchrack a few feet from Doc's animal.

"Hello," the man on the seat said. "Judd get himself a new deputy?"

Doc looked this man over. He was a tall, sun-browned man with a patrician bearing; a small mustache and goatee enhanced that impression. He looked like a Spanish don, and he dressed like one, but the man was no Spaniard.

"The old sheriff abdicated," Doc said gravely. "I appointed myself a deputy." He smiled at the look in the other's eyes. "The new sheriff is somewhere about," he added casually. "May I ask who you are?"

"You may," the man on the seat said sharply. "I'm Judge Henry Miller. And I don't like your high-handedness or your attitude, sir!"

Doc shrugged. "You should, Judge," he murmured. "You hired me."

Henry Miller stiffened. "You're Doc?" he whispered.

Doc nodded. "I reckon you've met the Kid."

Miller came down onto the walk and tied the gelding to the rack. He turned to Doc, his voice lowering. "What happened last night?"

Doc told him. "I don't know where the Kid is now," he said. He didn't feel it was any of this man's business why he had run out on the Kid last night.

Miller shook his head. "But Judd! In a cell!" He pushed past the Doc and surveyed the men in the cells. He walked to the one where Judd sat.

"You can't do this!" he snapped, whirling on Doc. "Judd's still sheriff here. You and Gary can't just take the law into your own hands—"

"Someone has to!" Doc cut in coldly.

Miller turned to the old lawman. "Judd—I don't understand this. But I'll see that you are set free. I'll get you out of here—"

"Don't promise anything you can't back up!" Doc warned. "He stays in there, until the Kid lets him out."

"I'll get a writ of habeas corpus," Miller said harshly. "I'll get in touch with—"

"You'll need more than a writ," Doc snapped. "You'll need a gun, Judge. And I don't think you can find one fast enough for the job!"

Miller settled behind his dignity. "You're making a mistake, Doc. You'll regret this." He turned his back to the self-appointed deputy and walked out. The gelding tossed his head as he untied him. . . . Miller climbed into the seat and swung the gig away from the sheriff's office. He rode out of town. . . .

Doc watched him go. This was the man who had hired them; this was the Kid's uncle.

Behind him one of the men in the cell with Sam Insted growled sullenly: "Well, Deppity—when do we eat? We got a right to three square meals—"

Doc turned, amused. "Well, well—a prisoner who knows his rights." He eyed the man, remembering him from last night, in Pedro's Café Reale. "The man from Gunsight. That right, Hank? Two years ago, in a gambling house called The Potluck—"

He turned and closed the door, and Hank Grogan swore harshly. . . .

The Casa Blanca was a square adobe building with narrow wrought-iron balustrades under the windows. It was the only hotel in Del Rio, although there were at least a half dozen boarding houses which would put up a stranger and feed him.

Doc crossed the strangely deserted square for the street running south. . . . The name painted in black on the side of the adobe building read: Main Street. He hesitated on the corner, looking for the restaurant he had noticed last night. . . . He was about to cross the street when the girl came out of the hotel.

He saw her look at him, and something in her attitude held him. He watched her come toward him, heels clicking sharply on the walk.

She was tall and shapely in a skirt and blouse whose soft tan color set off the clearness of her skin. Her gray eyes, he saw, were almost level with his. He took off his hat in a courtly gesture and she said, reddening slightly: "Are you—I have seen you with Gary Miller. Are you a friend of his?"

He nodded. "I have often thought of him as a son. And you—you must be Ann Vestry."

"Mrs. Sigleman," she said. "I am a widow." She smiled. "I was Ann Vestry before I married."

"I was about to have breakfast," he said. "May I buy you yours?"

She hesitated, glancing down the street toward Texas Square. Doc sensed she was thinking of her father, locked in one of his own cells. He said quietly: "We'll bring him some breakfast, too, Ann."

She nodded her acceptance. There was a sadness in her, a certain wistfulness. "I feel like a traitor to him. . . ." She looked at him quickly, and he introduced himself, smiling. "Gary Miller calls me Doc—it's all the name he knows. But you can call me Jonathan."

"I like Jonathan better," she said. "I do feel disloyal to my father. But if he were let out he'd kill Gary—or get killed!" She took a quick breath. "I don't believe Gary killed my brother, Jonathan. But my father does. He's never forgiven Gary for that night—"

"Perhaps you can tell me all about it over coffee, Ann," Doc suggested. He offered his arm and she took it, and the memories the gesture evoked were bittersweet. His face went wooden, hiding his feelings from her and whoever might be watching.

They went into the restaurant and found a secluded booth. . . . He listened to Ann while he picked at eggs and hashed brown potatoes. The Kid became real to him as Ann talked. In the years Doc had known the Kid, Gary had been a hard, self-contained man behind a fast gun. As he listened to this girl the Kid took on flesh and blood and he understood what had brought him back to Del Rio.

And he understood Judd Vestry, too. Living a lie. Walking a tight, narrow line against Yaegar. Keeping Yaegar's gun wolves at bay on the strength of a reputation no longer valid. . . .

He put his hand over hers across the table, and

there was nothing offensive in Doc's gesture. It was an impulsive gesture, meant to comfort, and he would have done it for his daughter, had he had one.

"Let's bring him some breakfast, Ann," he reminded. "And I'll try to talk to Judd again."

They went out. Ann insisted on carrying the tray. They crossed the sunlit plaza, skirting the softly murmuring fountain, and came up to the walk in front of the law office. And that was when Ann Vestry dropped the tray!

She let it fall from slackening fingers, her face whitening and distorting slightly with shock. Doc had his hand on the latch; he jerked in startled wonderment as the tray clattered on the boards. Coffee splashed over his boots and against his trouser cuffs.

He saw Ann's white face and her eyes widening with fear, and he turned slowly to see what had frightened the girl.

Mounted men were coming into the Square at a walk. Seven of them. Leading them was a hawk-nosed man Doc knew at once—a rider known by sight or description to every other gunslinger along the Mexican border!

Yaegar!

They swung around the fountain and headed for the sheriff's office, and Doc was suddenly conscious of the star he had pinned so boldly to his coat.

"Ann," he said firmly, "get away from here!"

Then he walked to the edge of the weathered boards and waited, knowing that at last his destiny had caught up with him. . . .

CHAPTER XI

The crew at Big Hat wakened early. But Gary Miller slept until the sun was high. He came awake to see Tom Blake's mustached face in the doorway of his bedroom. He sat up and looked quickly about the familiar room; from the slant of the sunlight through the window he knew it was late morning.

"You should have called me before, Tom," he said.

The Big Hat foreman shrugged. "We did a lot of powwowing last night. . . . Was near sunup when you turned in. Figgered you needed the sleep."

Gary ran his fingers through tousled hair. Foo Long, Big Hat's Chinese cook, peered around Blake, his moon face shining. "Bleakfast . . . dinner . . . allasamee. . . . You hungry?"

The Kid grinned. "Enough to eat a quarter of a Big Hat steer."

He rolled out of bed and dressed, combing his hair before the dresser mirror. This was his old room, whenever he had stayed over at the ranch. He had liked its Spartan furnishings far better than the heavily furnished room he occupied in the big house on the hill in Del Rio.

There was a dark stubble on his jaw, but he

decided to forego shaving. He washed and came out to the big kitchen where Tom Blake was waiting for him.

The ramrod sat with a mug of black steaming coffee in front of him, smoking a limp brown paper cigaret. He was all bone and gristle, molded by forty-eight years of sun and weather—a saddle-toughened, work-hardened cowman who gave to Big Hat a fierce and stubborn loyalty.

Gary slid into a chair across the table from him, and Foo Long brought him a platter of beef steak and eggs. The coffee pot was already on the table, and Gary filled his mug from it.

"Home-made biscuits, too," he murmured, as Long brought them in. The Chinese cook beamed. "You likee?"

Gary dug his elbow into the cook's soft middle. "You'll get me fat, like you, Foo—"

Foo Long giggled and retreated. Gary glanced at Blake, who shook his head. "I ate earlier."

He waited while Gary dug in, smoking, his face hard to read. Finally he broke the silence. "I'll take you around to meet the hands, Gary. Two-three of them you might remember. Bill Tate, Ollie Kemp and Art Lord. The others are new. 'Cept Larry Main." His voice held a strain of worry. "We've had trouble keepin' a crew since Yaegar moved into the Blackrocks."

"I didn't ask you last night," Gary interrupted, "but Uncle Henry said Dad left here

113

with Judd the night he was killed. Is that right?"

Blake nodded. "That was the day yore father brought the sheriff out to have a talk with me. I had run into some trouble on our south range. Some bushwacker got a slug through my right leg. That was just before we found out Yaegar had bought out the old Salters place and moved across the border into the Blackrocks. Next thing we knew there was wire strung along the south side of the river—and we began finding Big Hat steers that had drifted down that way shot." The ramrod's face held a dark flush of anger as he recalled the incidents.

"We told Judd about it and he shrugged it off. Said this trouble was out of his hands. Claimed he was getting too old to get mixed up in range trouble, and that the county wasn't furnishing enough money to hire extra deputies. He and yore father had an argument right here. They rode out together, but they wasn't speaking that night—"

Gary frowned. "You don't believe Judd killed Dad?"

"No!" Tom Blake's voice was harsh. "Judd's been acting mighty queer for some time now. But he wouldn't kill yore father. Not that way—not a knife in the back!"

Gary rolled himself a cigaret. "Yaegar?" It was a flat question.

The Big Hat ramrod shook his head. "Mebbe.

Or one of his men." He stood up. "Big Hat used to be a real spread, Gary. Could have become one of the biggest ranches in Texas. Before he died yore father was experimenting with Herefords and Brahmas. We were raising beef here. Now—" He reached for his hat on the prong by the kitchen door. "Come on—I'll show you what's happened."

They went outside and walked across the yard to the saddle shed. A short, wiry puncher Blake introduced as Lenny Simms roped a couple of horses from the corral and saddled them.

While Lenny was doing this Blake brought Gary over to the blacksmith shop and introduced him to the new smith. Larry Main was helping the cook out in the galley, and he nodded a greeting to Gary as he crossed the yard lugging firewood.

"Rest of the boys are out combing the brush by Badwater Springs," Blake said. "We'll ride over that way and introduce you."

Gary nodded. Then he remembered that Larry had mentioned that a Big Hat puncher had been killed last night—a youngster named Slim who had been talking with Jackson. He asked Blake if someone had notified him about Slim.

"Yeah. I sent Art Lord down to Del Rio with the wagon." He hesitated, his eyes cold and worried. "Used to be a time when Judd Vestry could handle things like that in town. He'd have the man who killed Slim in a cell—or on a slab beside

Slim." He shrugged. "I could take the boys to town—was thinking of it when you rode in last night. But I know what would've happened. We'd have gotten nowhere trying to find who killed Slim. And if we moved across the Square, into Yaegar's, we would have had a fight on our hands." His voice went sour. "A fight we aren't ready for, Gary."

They rode in silence for a long spell after that. Big Hat was in a shallow cup surrounded by low, grassy hills. Del Rio flowed through it, marked by a line of darker green.

Badwater Springs lay to the southwest, close by rocky, arid hills covered with brush and cacti. They were hot and barren hills, and they marked the southern boundary of Big Hat.

Gary and Tom Blake rode into camp where five men were earmarking a small gather of wild, lean steers they had combed out of the brush.

Gary recognized two of the sweaty, dust-caked punchers. Bill Tate, stocky, blond and turning gray. Ollie Kemp, rawboned, drawling and more bowlegged than Gary remembered. Gary shook hands with them and the new men, and Blake said, walking over to the hogtied steer by the ear-notcher:

"Take a look at him, Gary."

Young Miller looked the wild-eyed steer over. A scrawny animal, more Longhorn than Hereford, wild and tough. He turned to Blake.

"That's about the size of it," Blake said harshly. "We used to graze more than a thousand head around Badwater Springs. The year before yore Dad was killed we turned loose five hundred Herefords and a dozen blooded bulls. This is what we've been rounding up. We found three of the prize bulls shot. . . . We haven't seen hide or hair of the others."

"What about restocking?"

Blake sneered. "You might as well know, Gary. I was about to quit Big Hat when you showed up. Me an' yore uncle haven't been seeing eye to eye. He's blamed me for what's happened. Claimed I should have rounded up the bulls and brought them in to the ranch. Even went so far as to hint I might be in with Yaegar, helping him rustle our Herefords—"

"Uncle Henry!"

Blake nodded. "I never liked him, son. But he kept his nose out of Big Hat affairs when yore father was alive. When yore Dad was killed he took over. He rides out to the ranch once or twice a week in that red-wheeled surrey and expects to be waited on like some Spanish grandee."

Gary grinned. "Sounds like Uncle Henry. Reckon he should have been born a Castinado."

It was past noon and hot. Gary lifted his gaze to the surrounding hills. "Doesn't Felippe live over there?"

Blake followed his hand wave. "Yeah—back of that rock hill. Just east of the Shelf."

Old memories stirred through Gary. He knew these hills well—the hot draws and lonely box canyons—the shaded spots—the waterholes. He and Bob and Jose had hunted jacks and coyote and sometimes a cougar. Southwest of those broken hills was the *bosque* of the Rio Grande. . . .

Impulse moved him. "Let's ride up to the Shelf, Tom. I want to take a look at Big Hat from there."

Blake shrugged. They swung away from the hot, dusty camp and rode up a faint game trail which looped like some frayed brown ribbon across the slants of the steep, rock-mottled hills. The sun slid down toward the western horizon. They rode in silence, and the recollection came to Gary, in the hot stillness of these hills, of the men he had left locked in the sheriff's office.

He had forgotten about them—and about Judd. Forgotten, for the moment, even Ann. He had expected to remain in town; and the star he still wore on his shirt, and which Tom Blake had not questioned, had been his show of defiance to Yaegar and his killers.

By now, he was sure, Yaegar would have freed Sam Insted and the others. He wondered what they would have done with Judd. . . .

He was not yet ready for the showdown with

Diamond Cross. He glanced at Tom Blake riding slightly behind him. He knew the Big Hat ramrod would stand at his side against Yaegar. Tom was no green hand with the Colt he carried in the holster at his left hip, but he was not in the class with Yaegar, Sam Insted and some of the hardcases riding for Diamond Cross. Ollie Kemp, Bill Tate and Art Lord would probably stick, too; the fact they were still riding for Big Hat proved their stubborn loyalty. But how many of the new hands would he be able to count on?

He had come to Del Rio with Doc and Jackson. With these two men at his side he could have faced Yaegar. Without them . . . ?

He felt the loss keenly.

Glancing back to the distant Blackrocks, Gary felt the pressure of those men who had moved into them, to crouch like hungry wolves on the flank of Big Hat.

Something about the pattern of this trouble bothered Gary now. Yaegar was a wanted man in most localities along the Border. Why had Uncle Henry not called on the law? Granted that Judd Vestry had been unable, and seemingly unwilling, to keep order here, an appeal to the governor would have brought some sort of action. Why had Uncle Henry relied, instead, on men he had known only as notorious gunmen whose weapons were for hire?

They were coming up under the Shelf now, a

massive overhang of rock from which most of the valley of Del Rio could be seen. Many times, from its vantage point, Gary had spied on Big Hat; in these hot back hills which leveled off to the *bosque* of the Rio Grande he and Bob and Jose had played hare-and-hounds. . . .

They were climbing the steep pitch of the last hundred yards to the Shelf, and Gary turned to look back at Tom Blake. The gray he was riding slipped on loose rock and stumbled—and the whiplash of the bullet fanned Gary's cheek.

He heard the ugly splat of the slug hit Tom and heard the foreman grunt; then the rifle crack made its sharp detonation in the heated air.

Gary was out of saddle before his horse recovered its footing; he had his own Winchester cuddled in his hands. He levered a shell into position and fired and fired again, slamming his shots into and around the brush and rock where a faint puff of smoke marked where his ambusher had waited.

His bullets screamed in angry ricochet off the rocks, whining off into the heated stillness. He was firing blindly, he knew . . . but he wanted to give Tom a chance to crawl to safety.

There was no answering shot. He waited a while, stuffing fresh cartridges into the magazine. . . . Then he crawled through the brush to where Tom Blake lay, breathing heavily. The bullet had hit him high in the right side and was still in him.

Tom's horse had bolted. Gary's animal was down-trail, reins trailing. Gary crawled to it and caught the animal and led it back to Tom. He kept his Winchester ready, and his eyes searched that barren hillside for sign of movement. But he knew that whoever had fired that shot was gone.

He lifted the Big Hat ramrod into the gray's saddle. Blake sagged in the middle; his face was coffee-colored and his lips bloodless. He shook his head. "Can't hang on, son—"

Gary swung up behind his foreman. He held the Big Hat ramrod with his left arm while he kept the rifle steady in his right. He kneed the gray around and sent him down the treacherous trail.

They made it back to the camp by Badwater Springs in two hours. Tom Blake had gone slack against Gary's arm. The Kid's arm and shoulder muscles ached. He pulled up by the small leanto the Big Hat punchers had thrown up to provide some shade against the punishing sun.

Ollie Kemp came to his feet with a startled shout. Another puncher came to join him. They took Blake from Gary and lowered him to the ground, on the blanket they spread under the leanto.

Gary's mouth was a hard, thin line. "Fix him up best as you can, Ollie. Send a man to the ranch for a wagon and get another man to town for Doc Henderson—"

"Henderson's dead," Ollie muttered. "Drank hisself blind one night and fell off his buggy."

"No other doctor in town?"

"Sure," Kemp nodded. "A young feller name of Jones. Treffin Jones—"

"Get him!" Gary snapped. "I'm riding back—"

Ollie caught at the gray's bit. "Wait. Let me ride with you. Carter can go for the wagon and O'Connor will stay here with Blake. Bill and the others will be riding in soon—"

Gary shook his head. "This is my job, Ollie. The gent who shot Tom was trying for me. He's got a bad arm, or he wouldn't have missed by so much—" He was remembering Felippe lolling drunkenly on the seat of his cart, and the wagon piled high with loose straw. He knew now who had been in that wagon bed.

He swung the big gray away from Ollie. "Take care of Tom. And don't make any moves, no matter what the provocation, until I get back!"

Ollie nodded. His face was hard in the beat of the afternoon sun. . . .

CHAPTER XII

Yaegar and his men rode into Texas Square with the sun riding high. They came in armed, and in fighting formation, and Del Rio caught the warning and went still. Even the clamor of playing children hushed, as though suddenly anxious mothers had clapped hands to small, unheeding mouths. . . .

Yaegar saw the black-garbed man and the girl crossing the plaza to the sheriff's office. They were obviously unaware that he and his men were behind them. He turned slightly in the saddle of his big black and made his swift survey of the area and saw nothing to alarm him.

But Yaegar was a suspicious man.

He put his glance on the man and girl ahead as he wheeled around the fountain and saw them step up to the office. The man reached out to open the door and the girl idly looked back across the Square.

He saw her stiffen and the tray slid out of her hands. . . . It made a harsh clatter in the drowsy quiet of the plaza. Then the man in black turned and faced them, and Yaegar knew this man was Doc, one of the three gunmen known along the Mexican border as The Unholy Three.

He did not underestimate this man. Yaegar

seldom underestimated anyone. He put his bleak glance on this oldish man with the caved-in shoulders and the gun-hung holsters thonged to his hips.

Where was the Kid? He gave a sharp order heard only by the men with him. They swung into formation, like well-trained cavalry, flanking him and falling slightly back so that they made a shallow wedge with Yaegar at the point.

Doc had come to the edge of the plank walk, and Yaegar saw the glint of a badge on his coat and read the meaning of Doc's attitude. He was standing there, slightly crouched, his hands loose at his sides. Loose the way a man's hands are loose when he gets ready to draw. . . .

It could be that Doc and this girl were here as bait—that the Kid was waiting somewhere, gun cocked and ready. It might be a trap. Yaegar thought of this possibility and discarded it. The girl's reaction at sight of them, Doc's attitude now, indicated this had not been planned.

And the thought came to Yaegar that the Kid was probably out of town—might even have gone to Big Hat—and then it was past time for speculation.

He reined in less than fifteen feet from the spare, grave-faced man on the law office porch, and his voice was flat and cold. "Doc?"

Doc nodded slightly. He saw that Ann had moved away from him, out of the line of gunfire.

He glimpsed her white, drawn face as she paused, and wished he could have spared her this.

He knew Yaegar would be the man to kill him. The riders edging their mounts aside, giving him room, were an audience, stony-faced bystanders.

"Heard a lot about you," Yaegar said. He was drawing the moment out, giving the Kid time to make his appearance, if he was in town. "Always imagined I would run into you some day."

"All trails cross eventually," Doc murmured, "if a man rides long enough."

Yaegar smiled. "And all trails end somewhere, eh, Doc?" His eyes were narrowed now, cold and deadly with gathering anticipation.

"For you and for me," Doc agreed.

"For you," Yaegar corrected softly. "For you— and the Kid!"

"And Jackson?"

"Jackson's dead." Yaegar lied, but he wanted to see what effect this would have on Doc. He saw the barest flicker in the man's eyes, possibly a hint of sadness in the grooved mouth.

"The curtain's up, Yaegar!" Doc said harshly. He was being baited and he wanted no more of it. "The play's begun. And all trails end—"

He drew then, moving with all the speed he possessed. He was faster than Yaegar expected. He had one moment of satisfaction, seeing Yaegar flinch before the outlaw boss's bullets smashed into him, spinning him around like some wooden puppet. He fell across the hard planking in front of the law office, but he wasn't aware of it.

For Doc the end of the trail had finally come!

Yaegar cursed. It was a sharp outbreak of anger and pain. His left arm burned where Doc's bullet had torn across flesh; luckily it had not hit bone. He realized Doc had sacrificed aim for speed, but it was the first time an opponent's bullet had touched him, and it shook his arrogant confidence.

Ann Sigleman was still standing by the corner of the law office where a lane parted the building from the arcade beyond. He saw her lean against the side and close her eyes, and he dismissed her. His glance made an angry survey of the Square. He knew people were watching, but no one stepped out to interfere.

"All right," he growled to the men behind him. "Let's get the boys out."

They dismounted and clumped over the boards, ignoring the girl at the corner and the dead man by the door. Sam Insted was at the bars, waiting for them.

"Glad you came, Yaegar," he muttered. "Was that the Kid, or Doc, out there?"

"Doc," Yaegar answered bleakly.

He was conscious of the blood staining his bullet-torn sleeve, dripping down between the fingers of his left hand. He saw Sam's eyes widen, and he knew the thoughts that were passing through the mind of the Tombstone killer.

"Where does he keep the keys to that cell?" he asked coldly.

Sam grunted. "Kid took them with him—"

Yaegar turned and gave orders. Lariats were uncoiled, looped around the cell bars and tied to saddle horns. The boss of Diamond Cross stood aside as the animals lunged ahead to the quirt lashes of their owners. Rope stretched, sang. One parted, and the free end whistled through the air, slapping against the door frame, whipping against the glass and shattering it.

The iron frame of the cell front was anchored in wood. Under the terrific strain, the wood splintered and the framing tore loose; a section of the ceiling fell. The men in the cell crowded back against the rear wall.

The barred front clattered across the office, smashing the table and chair and sending the brass cuspidor skittering. Sam Insted stepped out, followed by the others. He went to the wall where his gun rig had been hung by Gary, and his eyes glittered as he strapped it around his middle.

The others trooped out and found their weapons. Baker, gingerly massaging the lump on his head, looked at Judd Vestry, sitting on the edge of his cot, watching them with remote interest.

"What about him, Yaegar?"

"Let him be!" Yaegar snapped. "He doesn't count!"

Anger showed on Judd's seamed face at the insult. But he sat there, watching them trample over the debris in his office, and knowing that this was the end of what he had stood for.

Yaegar said: "Here's Doc's badge," and tossed the nickel ornament to Sam Insted. "You're the law in Del Rio now, Sam! Make it stick!"

Sam's grin was vicious. "It'll stick!"

The gun boss stood in the doorway, looking over the wreckage. "I don't know when the Kid'll show up in town, Sam. I'll wait until sundown. Think you can handle him this time?"

Sam's eyes went murky. "Yeah."

Yaegar shrugged. "Hank, Baker and Keene will stay with you. I think we can all stand a drink. Meet me at the bar. I'm going over to Doctor Jones's office to get this arm bandaged."

He stepped out to the walk, ignoring Doc's body, and saw that Ann was still at the corner. She waited until Sam and the others came out; then she walked toward them and went into the office.

Judd Vestry stared at her. He stood up slowly as she came stepping over the debris to his cell.

"You didn't leave," he said. Then his eyes turned bitter. "Because of him?"

She nodded. "If you weren't so blind, Dad," she whispered, "you'd be on his side, against these killers—"

"Killers?" Judd's voice was stony. "He's a killer, too, Ann. It's you who are blind. He killed yore brother. And you stand there and tell me—"

She turned and walked away from him. Yaegar was waiting for her on the boardwalk. There was a small smile on his lips.

"Sam!" The gunman turned to him, frowning. "Escort Miss—pardon me, Mrs. Sigleman—to my place. The old Palacio Verde. See that she is treated like a lady. But see that she remains there, with you, until I get back."

Sam shrugged. Yaegar turned away and Sam walked to Ann, took her arm. "You heard the boss. Don't make me get rough."

Ann's eyes were angry. But she knew no one would interfere, even if she screamed and tried to get away from Sam Insted. Del Rio was afraid of Yaegar and his gunmen. . . . Del Rio called it being neutral.

She jerked her arm away from Sam. "Just keep your hands off me!" she said coldly. She walked across the plaza ahead of Sam, her head held high. . . .

Judd Vestry paced the confines of his cell. The bars of his own cubicle had been twisted by the tearing loose of the frame next to it. . . . He stopped by his door, and a sudden bitter frustration moved him into taking hold of the bars and shaking them.

The door opened.

He stared at it, not believing. It was as though an unseen power had answered his unspoken request. Then he realized that the warping of the entire cell front probably had twisted the lock, too, and sprung the bolt.

He pushed the door wider and stepped out. The outer door was open, but he could see no one on the walk outside. Yaegar and his men had gone, and the curious had not yet mustered enough courage to investigate what had happened here.

Judd stepped swiftly over the debris on the floor and found his guns. He slid them into his holsters, edged to the door, and glanced out. He saw Doc's body lying on the walk, a spatter of broken glass over him. A couple of mounted men were in the Square. Judd decided it was too risky going out that way.

He left the office through the rear door, stepping out to the alley and cutting back behind the buildings fronting the plaza. It took him five minutes to get to Zeke's Livery.

Zeke's part-time helper, Tootle, was in the barn, arguing with Zeke. Something about the unauthorized loan of a horse—the shiftless stable hand was sullenly offering to pay Zeke for it. Judd didn't bother to listen in on the argument.

He stepped into view, his hand on his gun butt. "Zeke!" he snapped. "I want a cayuse saddled.

Muy pronto. That big white stud with the black nose—"

Zeke stared at the sheriff. Tootle backed away from Judd, his sallow face congesting, as though the old lawman had lifted a threatening hand to him.

Zeke nodded. "Get that cayuse saddled for the sheriff!" he growled, turning to his hired hand. "Hurry it up and maybe I'll forget that horse you borrowed!"

He stood by, a heavy man with reddish sideburns that came down like a vise clamping his thick jaws. "Don't blame you, Judd, for skipping town—"

Vestry whirled on him. "Don't take this wrong, Zeke!" he snarled. "I'll be back. But I've got to kill a man tonight—at Big Hat!"

Zeke kept his counsel after that. He stood by while Tootle sullenly saddled the big white; he watched Judd step up into the saddle, nod grimly and duck low as he rode the horse down the manure-littered ramp.

Tootle licked his lips. "I'll leave now, Zeke—" He was thinking that Yaegar would like to know about Judd.

Zeke picked up the pitchfork leaning against the wall. "You'll stay awhile, Tootle!" he said harshly. "There's five stalls to clean out."

Tootle stiffened. "I'll clean them later—"

"Now," Zeke corrected grimly. He lifted the

131

pitchfork, and the tines seemed to fascinate the old bum.

"Sure, Zeke!" he gulped. "I'll give you a hand with them stalls."

Yaegar had his arm bandaged at Doctor Jones' office. The doctor went about the job with emotionless efficiency. Treffin Jones, M.D., was a lean, rangy man of around twenty-seven with a mop of tousled black hair he never seemed to comb. He had a brisk, cold manner of treating a patient—and a quick temper. He was known to have gotten into more than one fist fight over a political argument, or just a plain difference of opinion; he was one of the few men in Del Rio not afraid of Yaegar.

But he was no friend of the Millers, either; in the trouble brewing between Big Hat and Yaegar he was strictly neutral.

Yaegar said bluntly: "There's a dead man in front of the law office, Doc. You might be interested in him. He was a medic, too—or so he claimed."

Jones frowned. "I'm only interested in patients who are still alive. Dead men are in Moss Lake's department—he's the undertaker and coroner."

Yaegar grinned. "Thought you ought to know about this one. He called himself Doc. But he was better at killing than healing. Rather a silly name for a top gunman, isn't it?"

132

"Quite." Jones' voice was curt.

Yaegar had tried to get under this man's skin; now anger glinted in his gaze. He got up and tossed a double eagle on the table in a contemptuous gesture. "Buy yourself a couple of good cigars, Doc," he sneered, and walked out.

Treffin Jones picked up the coin. There was a red flush at the back of his neck. He tossed the gold piece onto the book case, and it fell behind the first volume of *Vanity Fair.*

He washed his hands and dried them and went out. He got to Doc's body a few seconds ahead of Moss Lake. A small group of the curious had already gathered. Some were poking around in the shambles of the law office. Jones bent over the dead man. In the hours since he had died, Doc seemed to have shrunk inside his clothes; he looked oddly insignificant.

Jones glanced at the undertaker. "I'll give you a hand with him, Moss. . . ."

Yaegar had walked back to his place. Sam and the boys were at the bar, their conversation loud and profane. Ann sat in a chair by the wall. Above her hung an oil painting of a Spanish lady, poised and proud. Whoever had painted that picture had caught some quality in his subject—a fusion of pride and passion in the remote and distant hauteur of those features.

And standing there in the doorway, Yaegar saw Ann for the first time. There was the same look in her as in the woman in the painting—but Ann was real. And old urges and desires welled up in him, surprising him with their intensity.

He had known women like Ann once—he saw how the years had made him callous. He was a proud man and an arrogant man—and until this moment he had not realized how lonely he was for a woman like Ann.

He walked slowly to the bar as Sam turned and hailed him, waving a bottle by the neck. He joined them and drank with them, but his thoughts were not with them and he didn't catch Sam's query the first time.

Sam repeated it. "Think the Kid'll show his face in Del Rio again?"

Yaegar looked at Sam. The Tombstone killer had an insolent sneer on his lips. Liquor seemed to bring out the chip on Sam's shoulder. But the man was no false-fronted badman. Sam lived up to his reputation.

He nodded. "Yeah—I think the Kid will be back. But I'm not waiting, Sam." He turned and looked at Ann with a long, thoughtful stare, and the girl stiffened and color smudged her cheeks.

CHAPTER XIII

Gary Miller rode with his guns loose in his holster. He went back up the trail toward the Shelf, but he left it before he topped the massive rock overhang. He rode between low hills that held the heat, his eyes searching the brush-covered slopes.

He knew it was Jose who had tried to kill him, and he knew where Jose would be headed. Eventually he came across a man's tracks in sand that was just firm enough to hold them. . . . He paused and saw where Jose had slipped climbing a small slope. And he noticed, too, that Jose was not alone. Someone wearing *huaraches* several sizes smaller was with Jose.

Gary's lips thinned. Carmelita was with Jose. It figured. Felippe was her father. He let his glance follow the marks of their passage as far as he could make them out; he knew now that if he had not gone back to the Big Hat camp with Tom Blake he would have easily caught up with them. For they were afoot.

And he knew where they were headed.

He put the gray on the trail and slid his Winchester out of his saddle boot. He rode easily, and just before sundown he sighted Felippe's shack.

There was a late afternoon hush in the hills, and the heat had a dry, brittle quality. The shadows were sliding down from the higher points into the ravines and draws, like soft and weightless blankets. Gary reined aside when he saw the dog break out of the bushes on the slope on his left, working silently and efficiently, and then the entire hillside seemed to come alive with bawling kids and goats. . . . They poured in a living flood toward the goat camp below.

A brown-faced boy of about fourteen, carrying a three-foot stick, was behind them; he was using the stick as a prod, turning the laggards. He saw Gary and went still, a brown statue in ragged clothing.

Gary touched heels to the gray and rode below the boy, following the drag of the herd, and pulled up by the door of the hut. The door was open, but it was gloomy inside and he could see no one. He held the rifle across his saddle horn, his face grim and expectant.

The hard-packed yard was littered with droppings. . . . The goats were still moving in a bawling, cavorting mass toward the open gate of the stone corral. He saw a small face peer at him from the door and disappear instantly as he turned his attention to it.

"Jose!" His voice was hard, ringing above the bawling of the goats.

Felippe came to the door. He wore the scowl

with which Gary was familiar. His eyes were bloodshot. Last night he had been a man without a care in the world; today he seemed to be carrying the troubles of the world on his back.

"No Jose," he said slowly.

Gary waited. Then he dismounted and, carrying his rifle held across his waist, walked to Felippe. The man made no move to get out of his way, nor did his expression change. "No Jose," he muttered.

The Kid pushed him aside and stepped inside the hut. It was small and cramped, and Carmelita's mother stood by the smoky fireplace, stirring in an iron pot. She didn't even look at Gary. But the four children in the room with her stared at him with big wide eyes.

Gary ran his gaze over the straw pallets in the one room and knew Felippe had not lied. Jose and Carmelita had come and gone. He came out and stood before the small man. "He was here, Felippe, with your daughter. Where did they go?"

Felippe shook his head. "Jose not here. No Carmelita." His voice was stubborn, and Gary knew he would get nothing from him.

The Kid swung away. Leading the gray by the bridle, he walked to the small shed behind Felippe's hut where Felippe's ox lay in an aura of sour fetidness, chewing placidly. The shed had another small hay bin in the opposite corner, and Gary spotted the droppings of a burro. They were quite recent, and he followed the sharp hoof tracks of this animal, seeing that they were intermingled with the imprints of a man's boots and a woman's *huaraches*.

He nodded slowly. Jose and Carmelita had gone, taking the burro with them. He saw that they were headed for the gap between the rocky hills behind the shack, and he knew where Jose and Carmelita were going.

He mounted the gray and slid the Winchester back into its scabbard. His face was as hard as the brown stones which dotted these barren slopes.

It was not going to be easy to ride Jose down, he thought stonily. Jose knew these back hills as well as he did, and he had Carmelita with him. The girl would slow him, but she would complicate matters, too.

His jaw ridged. This thing between Jose and himself had been a long time brewing—it had to be settled now.

Jose's trail vanished in the gap, obliterated by hundreds of sharp hoofs. A grudging smile touched Gary's lips. So that was what Carmelita's brother had been doing with his flock!

This would slow him. For behind this gap were a dozen narrow, twisting trails, all of them leading eventually to the Rio Grande. Jose could be taking any one of these.

The Kid played a hunch and headed for the

Funnel, a place where a narrow trail passed through naked rock that closed overhead, blotting out the sky. It was the fastest way through this broken country to the *bosque*, and he figured Jose would take it.

He guessed wrong.

The sun had gone down when he pulled up before the Funnel and looked for sign of Jose and the girl and the burro. He found none.

He looked toward the west, knowing now that his only chance was to cut across these low, rocky hills, hoping to cut Jose's trail somewhere yonder. But darkness came swiftly, and he turned the gray away, heading for a small waterhole he remembered.

When he reached it it was pitch dark. He dismounted and made a swift survey of the small spring on the off chance Jose might have doubled back here. Disappointment brought impatience; he forced himself to make camp here, knowing that any attempt to cut Jose's trail at night would be futile.

Graze was poor around the waterhole, but he picketed the gray on a twenty-foot line. Then he settled back and rolled himself a cigaret and stared into the night. . . .

Six miles to the southwest Jose Castinado had made camp. The burro cropped contentedly at spiky grass, his shaggy hide still damp from the day's travel. Night wrapped around them like a cloak.

The swagger was gone from Jose. His clothes were dust-caked and blood-stained and his dark cheeks were made darker by the stubble on them. His right arm was throbbing, giving him no ease; there was a feverish glint in his eyes.

Carmelita lay on the ground, her cheek pillowed on her arm. She was spent. She had insisted that Jose ride the burro most of the way; she had followed behind, stumbling at last through sheer tiredness.

It had surprised and dismayed her. Once she, too, had roamed these hills with tireless curiosity, with a girl's free-swinging stride and bright-eyed interest. . . . How many years since she had left home? How many years to put lead in her legs and shortness in her breath?

This mad flight—it could have been avoided. She had tried to argue with Jose. Gary did not even know Jose was here, at her father's place. But he had taken the old rifle of her father and gone scouting; he said he wanted to look at Big Hat from the Shelf. She had not entirely believed him, so she had gone along.

And Fate proved unkind. Two riders had appeared, climbing toward the rock overhang— and Jose had seen that Gary Miller was one of them. She couldn't stop him. He had missed— and this was the result.

Back at her father's hut, she had tried to argue

with him, and he had slapped her with dark fury. She had argued no longer. He was her man; she would stay with him. There was nothing in Del Rio to go back to—and long ago she had left the miserable hut of her birth.

Her feet ached and she moaned softly. And Jose, seeing her tired helplessness, felt a touch of pity. He knelt beside her and offered her water from his canteen.

She took it and drank, her senses dulled by fatigue.

"We'll rest here two, three hours," Jose muttered. "Then we travel. We must make the Rio Bravo before he catches up!" His eyes glittered dangerously. "He'll never find us, once we cross into Mexico."

She lifted her head. Her brass loop earrings glittered in the starlight, and her eyes held a faint hope.

"Perhaps he is not after us, Jose. Perhaps we are running from no one."

"He's after me!" Jose snapped. "I know Gary Miller." His lips tightened in bleak recollection; his voice was dry now, like the tearing of old paper. "It's between us, Carmelita—I feel it. Deep inside here—" He prodded his chest, and bitter anger twisted his mouth.

"I killed Bob Vestry—long ago. They thought I was their friend, Carmelita. But I hated them." He was looking into the darkness of the hills; he did not notice the strange look in the girl's eyes, the growing sadness.

"All the time I played with them I knew what I had to do. These hills, the valley of Del Rio— they belong to me! The Castinados made this their land—what right have the Millers to it? What right did Gary have to the land the King of Spain granted to my forbears?"

Carmelita made no answer to this, nor was an answer expected. Jose was no longer here at the moment. He was back in a time long gone, and the fever in his blood made the transport easy. He was seeing the column of marching men who had crossed the Rio Bravo a hundred odd years before to settle in the long valley of Del Rio.

"A stable boy!" he whispered harshly. "Me, Jose Castinado, a stable boy for the Millers!"

He was silent then, watching the marching figures fade into the darkness of the past, hearing the last jingle of silver conchos die in the night.

"I killed Bob Vestry that night. It was easy, Carmelita. We had planned to run away, Bob and Gary and I. What fools they were! We were boys. They hated the iron hand of their fathers. But I felt no iron hand, and had no desire to run away. Yet I planned with them that night—

"Pedro saw me, Carmelita. I think he knows. But he has never talked. I went upstairs and around to the veranda on the second floor. I looked through the window and saw Bob and

Gary arguing. They had been drinking while they waited for me. I think Bob was getting afraid. He didn't want to go. Gary called him a coward. And then I shot him."

Jose looked down at her and licked his lips. "I should have killed Gary then. But I got frightened, and ran. And then I waited for him to come back. I knew he would. I practiced long hours, Carmelita—I was sure of myself. And then—"

She put a hand on his left arm and pulled him down beside her. "Jose," she whispered softly, "you must rest. We will be on our way again in three hours."

He stretched out beside her, on his back. . . . She leaned over him and kissed him. His lips were cold and unresponsive.

Gary was up before the sun. He rolled out of his blanket and stretched and was instantly wide awake. He bellied down over the small pool and splashed cold water over his face and neck. A bird chittered in the brush; a pack rat scurried off through the fringe grass.

He found that the gray had stripped everything edible within picket range. He brought it to water, then saddled and mounted.

He had to run into Jose today, or the man would make it to the river. And there were too many *paisanos* in Mexico who would hide Jose. So

Gary pushed the gray through the early morning darkness and came across a game trail as the sun smeared the eastern horizon a misty pink.

He back-tracked along this faint path and found no sign of Jose and the girl and pushed on. . . . It was mid-morning before he found their sign. And it was noon when he came upon their dry camp of the night, and despair settled a hard hand on his shoulders.

He pushed the gray again, forcing it to a hard, brutal pace. Jose was hampered by the girl and a bullet-smashed arm. He would have to keep to the trail, the easier ways across these broken hills.

Some time later Gary reined in and gave the animal a breather. The heat was punishing him and the gray. The cayuse's tongue lolled and its flanks heaved like a giant bellows. Sweat made dark circles under Gary's arms, and his cotton shirt clung like mustard plaster to the small of his back.

"He's headed for the river at Comanche Crossing," he muttered. "That's the only way he can go now!"

It was treacherous country between here and the *bosque*. A jumbled stretch of eroded rocks thrust like spires into the brassy sky—coulees, washes, canyons that led nowhere. Even the Comanches had kept to the game trails when they fled this way into Mexico. . . .

Gary swung the gray across this broken land. He was playing a long shot this time, knowing that if he guessed wrong again Jose would be in Mexico while his bones bleached in the sun of some forgotten coulee.

The sun was low over the distant hills when he came across a stretch of malpais and halted on the rim of a steep break of land. And ahead of him he had his first glimpse of the man he hunted.

Jose was about a mile ahead, walking ahead of the tired burro. The girl stumbled along behind. . . .

He saw them stop and he knew he was seen.

A half-dozen miles ahead the river *bosque* made its dark and impenetrable barrier. Jose knew this section of the river as well as Gary. . . .

The Kid sent the gray plunging down the steep slant. The animal faltered and stumbled and Gary held his breath, his feet slipping free of the stirrups, ready to jump if the gray went down. But the iron-hearted animal regained its feet. It made the easier slant and plodded on now, head drooping, lather wreathing his muzzle like soap bubbles.

The figures ahead seemed barely moving, but even as he watched them they dropped out of sight. Gary dug his heels into the gray's heaving flanks and the animal picked up its pace, drawing on some reserve of strength.

He was coming up to the eroded cut in the

desolate land when he heard a shot. Gary flinched, a reflex action. The shot sounded close ahead.

He drew his right Colt and balanced it in his hand as the gray came up to the gully. His eyes sought the sand and gravel bed lying eight feet below. . . . He saw the burro standing with drooping head by the far bank, and a figure lay sprawled, facedown, a few yards away.

Gary's breath burned harshly in his throat; his lips felt swollen and dry as matchwood. He sent the gray sliding down the crumbly bank and slid out of the saddle.

Carmelita was moaning softly. He knelt beside her and turned her on her side, and his stomach tightened. The whole front of her cotton blouse was stained with blood.

Her eyes were glazed with fiery pain; she didn't recognize him. She thought it was Jose bending over her. Her lips quivered.

"Why, Jose, why? I only wanted to help. . . ."

She was looking up at him, past him, over his shoulder. Her eyes were focusing slowly, pushing aside the blur of pain. He saw them suddenly widen, and a thin scream racked her. *"Jose!"*

Gary twisted away. Jose's bullet smashed past his shoulder, into the earth so close to Carmelita that it tore the sleeve of her outflung arm.

Gary shot by reflex. He thumbed two fast shots at the blurred figure looming over the gully bank.

146

Jose screamed high in his throat. It died away. He twisted and flopped like a headless turkey. He came sliding down, still writhing, finally to lay still amid the rubble less than five feet from Gary's crouched figure.

Gary got to his feet. Carmelita's whisper turned him back to her. "Jose!"

He crouched by her. She was badly hurt—how badly he couldn't be sure. The bullet seemed to have entered her right breast. . . .

"Jose's dead," he said, and there was nothing he could add to that.

She closed her eyes. "I knew it would come to this." Her voice was strained. "He wouldn't listen to me. All I wanted for Jose was—" Pain knifed through her; her body arched, and a cry rose in her throat.

He took her in his arms. There was nothing he could do for her. She would be dead long before he could get her to a doctor.

"Jose killed Bob Vestry," she whispered. "He would have wanted you to know, now that he is dead. Pedro knows, too. Jose always hated you. . . . He hated all the Millers."

"Did he kill my father?"

Carmelita's head rolled limply. "I don't know—" Her body arched again with the terrible pain, and a sob came from her. "Holy Mother, forgive me—" Her voice faded; she seemed very tired. He held her in his arms and wiped the dust from her face, but she never spoke again. He held her until she died. He knew she was dead when a little tremor went through her. Then she was very still, and her weight had the strange inertness of matter no longer living.

The burro waited patiently as he lifted Carmelita's body across its shaggy back. The gray protested tiredly when he slid Jose's body across its saddle. Gary knew the gray would never make it back double-burdened. So he fashioned a loose hackmore for the burro with his rope and tied it to the gray's saddle horn. Then he took the gray's bridle and started walking.

It was going to be a long hike back to Big Hat.

CHAPTER XIV

Yaegar waited until sundown. He knew the Kid was not coming to Del Rio then.

Baker, who was not much of a drinking man, came into the saloon just as Yaegar had decided to leave.

"Judd's gone," he said. "I just checked in at the law office an' his door was open. Don't know who got him out. But he's not in his cell. An' his guns are gone, too."

Ann started. It was the only show of emotion she had shown during the afternoon. She had sat in stony silence, ignoring the men at the bar.

Yaegar saw the worry in her eyes and judged it correctly. It looked as if Judd would be taking care of the Kid for him.

Tootle pushed through the door a few minutes after Baker. He stood just inside, blinking, studying Yaegar and the men at the bar for a sign that he was welcome.

Yaegar waved him over. "Give him a drink, Frank," he told the man who was serving.

Tootle sidled up to the rail, a grin spreading across his dirty, gray-stubbled face. "Judd Vestry left town 'bout four hours ago," he announced. "I would have told you sooner, but Zeke put me to work—"

149

Yaegar nodded. "Where was he headed?"

"Big Hat," Tootle said. "He's ridin' that big white of Zeke's, an' he seemed in a powerful hurry. Said he had to kill a man."

Yaegar's smile grew wide. "Have another drink, Tootle." He was pleased with the way things had gone.

He turned to the Tombstone gunman. "I'm going back to the ranch. Think you can handle things in town, in case Big Hat rides in behind the Kid?"

Sam wiped his lips with the back of his hand. "Anything that comes from Big Hat I kin handle," he boasted.

Yaegar walked over to Ann. "You'll make a pretty house guest," he told her. "Not as fancy as Big Hat, but you'll find Diamond Cross hospitable, long as you behave."

Ann looked him in the eye. "Kidnapping a woman is a pretty serious offense, even in Del Rio," she told him coldly. "Perhaps my father is no longer capable of keeping order in town, but a wire to the governor will bring a company of Rangers—"

"Haven't you heard?" Yaegar said. "Your father's riding to Big Hat to kill a man. He won't be wiring anyone. And as for the offense—Mrs. Sigleman, you underrate me. You will ride out to Diamond Cross of your own accord. I will have a dozen witnesses who will swear that you came with me because you wished to."

Ann's lips tightened helplessly. "What do you want of me?"

"Your company," Yaegar said, bowing slightly. "And, should the need arise, you will make a beautiful hostage."

Her eyes flashed with deep contempt.

He smiled. "Shall we ride, Mrs. Sigleman?"

Ann got to her feet. Yaegar turned and called to the men at the rail, and the riders who had come to town with him pulled away from the bar. They tramped out ahead of Yaegar, mounting the animals tied up at the rack.

Doc's buckskin, which Yaegar had brought from the law office, nosed the rack, empty-saddled.

"Your mount," he told Ann coldly. "Doc won't mind—he's through riding."

They pulled away from the saloon while Sam Insted watched them, standing slack-bodied in the doorway, his thumbs hooked indolently in his cartridge belt.

Ollie Kemp missed the Diamond Cross contingent as he rode into town. He came in across the river, by way of the short cut; he had run his animal hard. He pulled up before the harness shop and dismounted, turning toward the flight of stairs leading up to Doc Jones' office.

Sam Insted's sneering voice stopped him. "Goin' somewhere, Big Hat?"

Kemp turned to face the gunman. He knew Sam

151

by reputation, and he knew he could not stand up to this man in a gunfight.

Sam had his right thumb hooked in his gun belt, three inches above the polished handle of his Colt. "Lost yore tongue?" he gibed.

"I've come for Doc Jones." Kemp's voice was thick. "Tom Blake got shot this morning—"

"You don't say?" Sam's voice held a heavy sarcasm.

Kemp licked his lips. Sam was baiting him, he knew. The man would not let this thing go without forcing trouble. A cold knot formed inside Kemp's stomach.

"I don't want trouble, Sam," he said harshly. "Blake's in bad shape. He needs the doc right away."

"Now ain't that a shame," Sam sneered, "seein' as how I just put out an order that all Big Hat riders will be jailed as soon as they ride into town!"

Kemp stiffened. "You can't do that—"

"Who says I can't!" Sam's voice was vicious now, all pretense stripped from it. "Heck with yore ramrod, fella! Yo're not goin' to see Doc Jones. Yo're headed for the inside of a cell."

Ollie made his play. He was slow. Sam drew and jabbed the muzzle into Ollie's stomach, and when the man jackknifed he slammed him over the head. It was the way the Kid had treated him, and he felt a grim satisfaction as Kemp slumped.

Ollie went down to his hands and knees and was sick. He lay half dazed.

Sam chuckled. "Changed my mind, Big Hat. You kin go in an' see Doc Jones. When you get back to Big Hat, give that *muy malo hombre* who calls himself the Kid a message from me. Tell him I'll be waitin' for him alone, on the stairs in front of Yaegar's Saloon. Tell him, fella!"

Ollie Kemp was too sick and hurt to make any reply. He was hardly aware of it when Sam turned on his heel and stalked off. He pushed himself to his feet a bit later, with great effort, and wiped his face with his neckerchief. He was still green around the mouth, and his eyes had a yellowish glaze.

"I'll tell him, Sam," he whispered, but it was an effort to talk. "An' I want to be with Gary when he comes for you—"

He dragged himself up the long flight of stairs to the doctor's office. Doc Jones, he found, was out. He waited, sitting on the black horsehide settee, his mind fuzzy, until Jones returned.

He told the young medic about Tom Blake, and Jones took a deep breath and pushed hair from his eyes. "Looks like Moss Lake and I are going to be about the busiest men in Del Rio for a spell—" He turned and thumbed through his black book on his desk. "No urgent calls tonight." He nodded briskly. "I'll have my buggy out front in ten minutes."

● ● ●

Judd Vestry made Big Hat about the time Yaegar was leaving Del Rio with his daughter. He rode into the ranch yard which had often seen him as a friend; he rode now with a gun in his hand and a bleak and unyielding hate in his eyes.

The Big Hat punchers clustered about the shed and bunkhouse turned to face him. Hands dropped to gun butts, and a battery of hostile eyes targeted the old sheriff as he reined to a stop by the ranch-house.

Art Lord came out to the veranda. Art had been with Big Hat a long time; he knew why Judd was here.

"The Kid ain't here, Judd!" he said clearly. Then anger roughened his voice. "We got a wounded man inside—Ollie's headed for town for the doc. I got no time to waste with you, Judd!"

Vestry's voice held an iron harshness. "You'll take time, Art! Just send Gary out. I'll give him a chance—more of a break than he gave my son!"

"Yo're a fool!" Art snapped, and saw Judd's gun hand quiver. "Tom Blake was shot up by the Shelf. Gary was ridin' with Tom." He measured the hate in this old man who had once been Dwayne Miller's closest friend. "The Kid's out there now, huntin' the man who shot Tom—"

"Yo're lyin'!" Judd snarled. His eyes shifted to the man who came out of the ranchhouse to stand beside Art.

Larry Main's voice held acid contempt. "All hell's breakin' loose in Del Rio, Judd, an' all you can think of is the man who shot Bob! Yo're not even sure it was Gary Miller. You couldn't be, if you kept an open mind about it. I'll tell you somethin', Judd. I've been hangin' around in town for more than a week. I've heard a few things. Things you might have heard, too, if you wasn't so muleheaded in thinkin' Gary killed Bob."

"You talk too much, Larry," Judd sneered. "No wonder Henry Miller fired yuh." He started to turn the big white; Larry's voice came after him, sharp and jogging him.

"Ask Pedro to tell you who killed Bob! Stick a gun in his belly, if you have to! But get him to tell you!"

Judd jerked around, his face whitening. "What does Pedro know that he hasn't already told me?" he snarled. "Pedro was the man who swore he saw Gary kill Bob!"

"Ask him now!" Larry challenged. "Tell him Jose's good as dead, an' he don't have to worry any more if he tells the truth! Ask him, Judd!"

The old sheriff's eyes held distrust. He was not convinced. "I'll ask him," he muttered, "after I have it out with Gary Miller!"

He jerked the white around and sent it running out of the ranch yard. Art Lord started down the stairs after him. "By heaven," he swore, "I've had enough of the old fool! I'm goin' after him—"

"Let him ride, Art!" Larry said. "He'll never rest until he finds Gary. He's not the ambushin' kind, so it'll have to be face to face. An' if that's the way it has to be—"

Art threw up his hands. "Aw, to blazes with him!" he said disgustedly, and came back up the stairs. He flung a last look toward the trail to Del Rio. "Hope Ollie doesn't run into trouble in town. I don't like that slug in Tom. . . ."

Judd Vestry rode south, toward the Shelf. It didn't occur to him not to believe Art Lord. Gary was out here somewhere, but sooner or later he'd have to ride back.

Common sense clamped a lid over his boiling impatience. He made camp as soon as it got dark. He wasn't sleepy. He sat cross-legged, looking into the darkness, waiting for morning. . . .

Judd was in saddle at daybreak, riding slowly, his eyes ranging the hills. He knew this country and the trails which led to the Rio Grande. He found Gary's trail under the Shelf and followed it to Felippe's.

The old goat herd was taciturn, but he nodded eventually under the sheriff's cold prodding.

"*Si*—Jose was here. With Carmelita. They took my burro an' left. They were going to Mexico. That Meeler boy came after—he wanted Jose—"

Judd swung away. It was noon when he caught sight of Gary leading two burdened animals. He drew quickly off the trail, behind screening mesquite, and lifted his Colt from holster. His mouth held angry bitterness, but there was a flicker of doubt in his eyes.

Gary plodded up the trail. Behind him the gray suddenly held back on the bridle and snorted softly, his ears pricking forward. Gary came alert, his hand dropping to his gun butt.

Judd's cayuse brushed branches as he came out to the trail in front of Gary. The sheriff's voice was harsh. "This time I call the play, Gary!"

He stood over Gary, twisted in the saddle, his Colt cocked. Gary stared at him. He didn't know how Judd had gotten free, and all of a sudden it didn't matter. His hand slipped off the sun-warmed butt of his Colt, and he stood with arms loose at his sides.

"Still think I killed Bob, eh?" he muttered. "You've got a wooden block for a head, Judd, and nothing I or anyone else can say will ever convince you." Anger at the man's blindness shook him; anger at the harm this man had done himself and his daughter because of this thing.

"All right, shoot! Get it over with! Go back to Del Rio and sit behind that desk of yours and feel righteous, Judd! For six years you've waited to get the man who killed Bob—now you've got your chance!"

Judd's gunhand trembled. "You deny it?"

"You pigheaded fool!" Gary snarled. He was

past caring now about this man's feelings. "I've always denied it. But you and Dad had it all figured out. I was a wild kid who gave Dad trouble, and to you I was a bad influence on Bob. So you believed what you wanted to believe. You and my father rode out to the big house on the hill that night ready to hang me; you wouldn't have listened to anything I might have said!"

Judd's face was white. He knew Gary was right. He brushed his free hand across his eyes.

"We would have listened to you, son," he muttered. He wanted to believe Gary now; he had always thought of himself as a fair man. "It wasn't the way you think. Yore father an' I would have listened. Sure, I was blind crazy when I found Bob dead in that room. And Pedro swore you were the only one in that room with Bob. He said he'd heard you arguin' with him. An' then you ran away, son. I guess that kinda cinched it for me—an' for yore father, too."

"Jose killed Bob!" Gary cut in harshly. "That's the truth! Carmelita told me before she died. But you'll never believe it—"

"Maybe I will," Judd muttered. He lowered his Colt wearily, like a man coming to the end of a long road and looking forward to resting. "Maybe I should have listened to Ann, an' to Larry Main when he told me to ask Pedro again."

He took a long, shuddering breath. "Why did Jose do it?"

158

The anger went out of the Kid, leaving him strangely spent. He told Judd what had happened. "Reckon Jose always hated me," he finished, and there was still a thread of wonder in his voice.

Judd roused himself. He recalled what had happened in Del Rio, and he told Gary of Doc's stand. "I couldn't see it from my cell, son. But I reckon he stood up to Yaegar an' lost out. He nicked Yaegar, though. There was blood on Yaegar's left arm when he came into the law office."

Gary was stiff again, his jaw grim. So Doc had come back. Had taken up where Gary had left off. Had faced Yaegar alone. . . .

It was time he got back to Del Rio.

Judd said wearily: "They've laughed at me, Gary—all the while I thought they were leavin' me alone because they were afraid of me! But they were laughin'. I know that now." His eyes mirrored his self-contempt. "Yaegar's in Del Rio, Gary, waitin' for you. I won't be much help. But I'm ridin' back with you, son!"

Gary shrugged. "This is what I came to Del Rio for, Judd. There won't be peace until this thing is settled!"

Judd made a motion with his hand. "Ride up behind me. This big stud can carry double—"

They made Big Hat just before midnight. They rode into the yard and saw that a light was still burning in the ranchhouse. A buggy was parked by the corral.

Shadowy figures appeared in the bunkhouse doorway. A voice hailed them grimly.

Gary said: "It's me—and the sheriff!" He dismounted, and Judd slid down beside him. Grim-faced punchers came out to them, stared at the bodies. One of them answered Gary's tired question.

"Yeah—Doc Jones is still inside—"

Gary and Judd went into the ranchhouse. Blake was in his bed, his eyes closed, breathing slowly. Doc Jones dozed in a chair by the bedside.

He woke at their footsteps.

"I'm Gary Miller," the Kid introduced himself. "How's Tom?"

Jones shrugged. "I'll know in the morning." And then, seeing the look in Gary's eyes, he said gruffly: "I think he'll pull through."

Gary turned away. There was nothing he or Judd could do here. "Better get some sleep," he told the sheriff. "We'll ride early tomorrow."

CHAPTER XV

Yaegar personally directed the preparing of breakfast that morning. Joaquin, his fat Mexican cook, usually had breakfast ready before he called Yaegar. But this morning the boss of Diamond Cross was up early, grooming himself with careful attention.

Joaquin was setting the table. Yaegar walked over to Ann's door and knocked. He knew she was awake. He had heard her moving about in the room an hour earlier.

"Breakfast," he announced pleasantly.

She made no answer.

"Ann," his voice was careful, "you may have heard many things about me. Some of them, unfortunately, may be true. But I have never harmed a woman. I wouldn't lay a hand on you unless you wanted me to. Nor will I allow any man who works for me to treat you as less than a lady."

He waited, controlling his impatience.

"Ann! I want to talk to you!"

He heard her come to the door. Furniture rasped across floor boards. He stepped aside as the bolt snicked back and Ann opened the door.

She was dressed and her face was drawn. There was a tired look in her eyes, and a quick searching scrutiny.

He bowed and waved her to the table where Joaquin, his broad face beaming, was standing by.

"It's not the St. Charles of Philadelphia," he said, "nor Henri's in New Orleans. But the eggs are fresh laid this morning, or Joaquin and his chickens will answer to me. And the coffee tells its own story."

Ann walked to the table, which had been covered for the occasion with a gay-colored tablecloth. Yaegar stepped quickly behind her and eased the chair for Ann to sit. He was every inch the suave gentleman this morning. He had shaved carefully and added a bit of cologne; he had dressed in an expensive suit and frilled shirt. And as an added touch, because he thought it would look romantic, he had put his bandaged arm in a black silk sling.

Yaegar wanted this woman because she stood for something he knew he was missing, a woman's graciousness and quality sheathed in the steel of pride.

He poured her coffee, feeling exhilarated and gay.

"It's been years since I've known what it is to have breakfast with a lady," he confessed. "Usually I have Sam or one of the boys in here. Most often I eat alone. I've missed something, Ann; something I've just come to realize is more important than money or power." He watched her face, hoping for a break in her stony, watchful regard; he put his hand over hers, holding it lightly.

"Ann—I've missed you—"

"You've seen me a hundred times," she said coldly. She didn't try to draw her hand away, but it was cold and unresponsive under his palm.

"No," he said, smiling. "I saw you only yesterday afternoon, as you sat under the painting of *Doña* Alva Aragon. Miguel Aragon had taste and style—that's why I bought him out. But my men aren't the type for frills—"

"One of your men killed my husband," she reminded him.

He pulled his hand back, his eyes somber. "Slim Trevor acted on his own, not on my orders, Ann."

She shook her head. "And Dwayne Miller—?"

"I didn't kill him, contrary to town opinion," he retorted. His voice was rough now, edged. "Ann—I'm not spotless. I won't attempt to picture myself to you as such. This is a violent land, and a man learns to hold up his end here, or he doesn't last. This is a country where the muzzle end of a Colt makes the final decisions. I've learned to make mine a bit faster than most, that's all. Money is still the prime ingredient of power, here as well as in the East. I want power, Ann. Any man with brains and ambition wants power. Here land plus cattle equals power—and I'm going to get both!"

163

"By taking it from someone else?" she said. Her voice was flat, but there was an edge of contempt to it, and he reacted to this.

"Dwayne Miller took it from Juan Castinado and old Juan's ancestors took it from the Indians. A king six thousand miles away signs a paper giving a certain Spanish subject a thousand square miles of land in a country he's never seen—where did the natives count in this?" He was angry now, and his argument had the force of complete belief. "Sure, Dwayne Miller bought Big Hat and the house on the hill from Juan. For a few thousand dollars—less than a tenth of what it was worth—"

"But he bought it," she pointed out. "He acted within the limits of the law."

"The law?" He sneered at this. "Who was the law? Who stood up for Juan Castinado's rights in the transaction? He was beyond caring what happened to Big Hat—he didn't even remember he still had a son. Did anyone consider him at that moment? Dwayne Miller didn't. He saw his chance to get Big Hat for almost nothing and he pushed the transaction. Sure, it was legal—on the surface."

"In the eyes of the law Big Hat belongs to the Millers," she said firmly. "Killing won't give you Big Hat. Using your guns against Gary Miller won't transfer Big Hat to you—"

"Perhaps not," he said abruptly. He leaned back, his composure restored. He smiled a little. "It may be that I will not have to kill Gary. Your father will do that for me."

He saw her face whiten, but her eyes remained cold and unfriendly. And now he wanted to break through that coldness; quite suddenly he wanted to hurt this woman whom he could not reach.

"Right now your father is probably dead—with Gary's bullets in him. Or else Judd has killed the Kid!"

He got what he wanted, and more. He saw now that he would never own this woman. That she already belonged to someone else. That she had always belonged to Gary Miller, in spirit—and that Mort Sigleman had been cheated.

He brushed his cup aside and stood up, his face mirroring the dark hurt to his pride. For a moment the suaveness was stripped from Yaegar.

"I hope it's Judd who's on the wrong end of a bullet!" he snarled. "Because I want to kill Gary. And when I do I'll come back here—and I'll take you, Ann, and I'll break you!"

He walked out of the room and stood on the shaded porch, feeling a dark and ugly mood build up in him. He wanted to kill Gary Miller!

Big Hat lay out of sight behind the swell of ground to the northwest. Big Hat, he decided grimly, was due for a visit. The time had come to drop all pretense.

He gathered his men. He left one rider, Reno, to stand guard over Ann. "Keep her in the bedroom, and keep your hands off her!" he warned. "If she makes trouble, slap her! But otherwise leave her alone!"

He looked in the bunkhouse where Jackson was still tied to his chair. The big man had his back to the door. He seemed to have sagged lower down; his head was resting on his chest. He didn't even stir at Yaegar's sharp order to the redhaired man lying on his bunk.

"Red—I want you with me. We're raiding Big Hat!"

Becker swung his feet to the floor and glanced at Jackson. "What about him?"

"Do what you want with him!" Yaegar snapped. "But finish it fast!"

Red grinned. "Sure. Go ahead, boss. I'll catch up—"

He walked to the door and watched Yaegar and the others ride out of the Diamond Cross yard. He waited until they were out of sight. Then he turned back to the man tied in the chair.

For two days Jackson had lived in a daze of pain and hate. Except for certain necessary functions, he had lived in that chair, eaten and slept in it. Stripped of privacy, humiliated, tortured, he had clung to one impossible hope—to live long enough to get his hands on Red Becker!

And in those two days he had remained unbroken in spirit and grim determination.

In a dozen ways Red Becker had tried to smash this man—make him crawl, sob out for mercy. He had tried fire and ridicule, humiliation and violence; he had tried painting again the picture of desecration, although the memory of that event had dimmed in Red's mind and he had to recreate it out of imagination and cruelty.

And all the while Jackson had worked at his bonds. Each time he was untied and retied he gained a fraction of an inch. Each time he felt closer to the moment he could break free. . . .

Now he looked up and watched Becker loom over him. Vaguely, as from another world, he seemed to have heard Yaegar tell someone outside the bunkhouse to stand guard over a girl in the ranchhouse. . . .

Becker chuckled. "Yaegar said to make it fast, Jackson. But I'm in no rush." He slid his sheath knife free and held it in front of Jackson's face. "An ear first. A piece of you at a time. You'll scream, Big Boy. You'll scream and beg before I get through—"

Jackson spat in his face. The spittle ran down the bridge of Red's nose, and murder flared across the sadistic killer's vein-ruptured face. He reached out and took hold of Jackson's left ear and severed it with one downward sweep of the blade.

Blood came in a small spurt down Jackson's neck and a tight sound, like a forced mewing, sounded in his throat. He lunged hard against his bonds and felt one strand slip over his knuckles—

Becker stepped back and wiped his face. "The other one next!" he snarled. "A piece at a time—"

Jackson was a wild man, straining, his veins knotting at his temples. His huge shoulders bunched and the chair creaked—and then he had his hands free, and he was lunging for Becker. Jackson's legs were still tied to the chair—he couldn't have caught the killer if Becker had moved in time. But Becker seemed frozen by Jackson's freedom. When he did move it was too late.

Jackson's big right hand clamped around his throat, jerking him down. Becker brought his knife around in one spasmodic thrust and felt it sink into the big man's side; then he lost his hold on it as he was twisted and brought down across Jackson's knees.

The sturdy chair creaked and threatened to fall apart under the extra weight. Becker was bent back across Jackson's knees, like some piece of firewood. Jackson's face was smeared with blood; he was breathing heavily, his eyes glaring with a wild and unheeding fury.

Becker tried to scream. But the fingers digging into his throat throttled all sound, all breathing. He threshed helplessly, and Jackson brought his enormous strength behind his arms. Something snapped in Becker's back and neck. His body convulsed and went limp.

Jackson let him slide to the floor. He felt pain now, burning and tearing his side, stabbing his groin. He wiped his face with the back of his hairy arm.

Becker's knife lay by the chair. He picked it up and cut himself free. There was a faint roaring, as from a lynch-mad mob, in his head. He staggered blindly, and there was only one thought left in him—to destroy!

He found the oil lamp on the wooden shelf in a corner, and a box of wood matches beside it. He swept the glass chimney to the floor and emptied the coal oil over the bunk and tinder-dry floor boards. His fingers fumbled with the matches. Finally he lighted one and dropped it on the bunk and stared in dazed anticipation until the flames leaped up to scorch his face.

Then he stumbled toward the door. The white beat of sunlight hurt his eyes. He lurched across the yard, still holding Becker's bloodstained knife in his hand. He stumbled up the stairs, fell, and left a bloody hand print on the boards. He jammed his heavy shoulder against the door and caught Reno with his feet on the kitchen table, reading an old *Farmer's Almanac*.

If an elephant had walked in waving a Confederate flag, Reno would not have been more shocked. He stood frozen, his eyes popping, while Jackson located him through a bloody blur and lunged for him. Reno's exclamation choked in his throat. He jerked his feet down to the floor and kicked his chair aside as he drew and shot at the charging man.

The bullets slammed in Jackson; they did not stop him. He brushed the small kitchen table aside and slammed into Reno. The wiry gunman smashed into the wall at his back and Jackson pinned him there, a slab of a hand finding his throat. The other used the knife—

Through the terrible roaring in his head Jackson heard a woman scream. He turned and let the bloody thing in his hand slide limply to the floor. He wiped his eyes and saw, seemingly far away and wavering, a girl in a doorway.

He waved his hand to her. "Get out of here." The words were thick and savage in his throat. He started to walk to her, and she turned and ran. Jackson stumbled over the overturned table. He groped around the room until he found a lamp, poured oil over the wall and floor. He found a match and scraped it into flame. He bent slowly, nursing that small fire, and then the match slid from his fingers and he collapsed.

A bluish puff circled Jackson's limp body and raced toward the oil-soaked wall. . . . Thirty seconds later flames were licking toward the window.

Joaquin, dozing in the shade by the spring, was

startled out of his siesta by the shots. But he arrived too late. When he reached the house it was already burning beyond control—and the bunkhouse was a mass of smoke and flame.

He stood open-mouthed, wondering what had happened. Then he heard a rider behind him and turned to see Ann Sigleman ride out of the corral.

Joaquin made no move to stop her.

CHAPTER XVI

The first hot rays of the sun warmed the faces of the hard-eyed men saddling horses at Big Hat.

Tony Armillo, who had a wife and six children living in a hut just outside Del Rio, stood by the tool shed, a pick and shovel by his side. Gary had ordered him to stay behind, as he had told Larry Main. And there was Ned Sewell, the big blacksmith, who had recently married and whose wife was expecting.

They had orders to bury Carmelita and Jose Castinado over by the river. Once this land had belonged to the Castinados—it was the least he could do for Jose.

The others were all single men, and of these no one backed out. Art Lord and Ollie Kemp were bachelors and old hands, and so was Bill Tate. Pete Nixon, Nosy Edwards and an eighteen-year-old hand who called himself Al Smith completed the Big Hat contingent.

Judd Vestry mounted Zeke's big white stallion and swung in beside Gary. He had slept little in the hours before dawn. He had tossed and turned, plagued by regrets that were vain— haunted by a fear for Ann's safety.

They wheeled away from Big Hat with the sun less than two hours high. Larry Main and Doc

Jones watched them from the ranchhouse steps.

Doc Jones shook his head. He was thinking of the strange irony of this thing: that while he fought to save a man's life these men were riding to kill. . . .

Gary rode the long miles to Del Rio in bitter silence. Ollie had relayed Sam's challenge to him, and he knew that Big Hat's survival depended on the outcome of what happened today.

His shabby treatment of Ann bothered him now. He had left her with the promise he'd see her again, and then had departed that same night for Big Hat without leaving word. He glanced at Judd's stony face and knew that Ann was on the sheriff's mind, too . . . and he felt sorry for the lawman.

The road followed the river for several miles before it cut away from the meandering stream to loop across rolling hills. It met the river again just outside Del Rio, and here Gary pulled up, the others clustering about him.

It was past noon; most of Del Rio would be having their siesta. But Sam would be waiting. The Tombstone killer had a reputation to live up to—or die for. He would be waiting, as he had told Ollie, on Yaegar's stairs.

But it was Yaegar and the rest of the Diamond Cross hands who worried Gary. By reputation, the Diamond Cross gun boss was not the kind of man to let another man do his fighting for him—

and this was Yaegar's fight. But Sam had issued the gun challenge. It could mean that Yaegar had decided to let Sam be the bait that would bring the Kid to town. And if Sam lost out, Yaegar's guns would still be there. . . .

"We'll split up here," he decided. "I'll ride in alone to take Sam. The rest of you swing around and come into Texas Square by way of the alley flanking the law office. Wait out of sight of the plaza. If Yaegar's holed up in his place, we'll give him a fight. But I'll draw Sam out first."

"I'm riding with you," Judd said. There was a deep stubbornness in the man. Gary shrugged. They waited while the six Big Hat riders swung away. And then Gary reached up for the badge he still wore on his shirt.

"Never should have taken it away from you, Judd," he said. He held it out, and Judd took it and slid it into his shirt pocket.

They rode together across the river, into Del Rio where Sam Insted was waiting. They rode in silence now; all that needed to be said had been said.

Word ran ahead of them, like the signal beat of tom-toms. It reached Sam Insted, smoking a panatella in Yaegar's. The Tombstone killer looked at Hank and Keene and Baker, his cellmates of the night before, and said: "I'll take care of the Kid. If anyone else horns in, back me up!"

Tootle, who had brought the news to Yaegar's,

shook himself like a hound dog with fleas. "Just the Kid an' old Judd, Sam. Don't make sense. I thought Judd was out to kill the Kid?"

Sam didn't make sense out of it, either. But he didn't care. He had sent his challenge to the man who had humiliated him in Pedro's Café Reale, and now he'd have his crack at the Kid.

No man had ever had a second chance at Sam Insted.

He pushed a half-filled bottle of whiskey to Tootle, who snared it deftly. "Take it an' git," Sam told the stable bum, "before you get in the way of a stray slug."

Tootle scuttled to the door. He glanced across the Square to the point where Main Street started, and in that moment Gary Miller and Judd Vestry rode into view. Tootle's shoulders twitched. He headed away from them, running under the shadowed arcade, and finally stopped when he ran out of breath. He was at the end of the building line, where a narrow alley separated him from the sheriff's office. He stopped here and waited, turning his attention to Yaegar's, where Sam Insted had appeared. . . .

Gary Miller saw the man as he turned into Texas Square. He saw Sam lean indifferently against the adobe pillar flanking the stairs, and for a brief instant he felt the icy hand of doubt touch the back of his neck.

Sam Insted was a fast gun. As fast as Jose?

Judd glanced at the Kid and saw the hard line of his jaw, the bleak and dispassionate look in his eye. Dwayne Miller's wild boy, he thought, and remembered that this man was the Kid, rated one of the deadliest men on the Border.

The sound of their horses' hoofs rang on the rough cobbles of the Square. Sam waited. The cigar burned slowly between his lips. When Gary and Judd were twenty feet from him, he took the cigar from his mouth and dropped it at his feet.

Gary reined Jackson's big gray to a stop. Judd eased his mount away, putting a space between them. He clasped both hands around his saddle pommel and leaned forward, his eyes searching the windows behind Sam.

"You want me, Sam?" Gary's voice slanted down at the gunman.

Sam's head jerked toward Judd. "See you brought the old man along, Kid. You figger you gonna need help?"

Judd's mouth went hard at the insult. But he kept silent, his hands tight on the pommel. His attention was on the blurred figure he glimpsed at the window behind Sam.

"I don't think so, Sam," Gary said. His voice was level, curt. "I didn't need help in Pedro's—"

Sam's eyes went murky. "You'll need it now!" he snapped. "But Jackson's probably dead—an'

Doc is colder than last year's ice. There's only you left, Kid—"

Across the Square Tootle had been edging toward the alley; he heard a horse snort, and curiosity pulled him to the corner for a look. He saw the riders waiting, and he whirled and yelled to Sam: "Big Hat riders—"

Sam moved. It was as if Tootle had touched a spring release in him. He spun away from the pillar and drew and shot in a blinding continuous motion.

The Kid had dismounted. He stood to one side of the big gray, crouched behind his own gun. He felt the whiplash of Sam's first bullet, and then Sam's second shot sent the animal rearing, shrilling with pain.

Sam stumbled out of his own gunsmoke. He had both guns in his hands, but the muzzles sagged downward. He came up on his toes, slanting a long bleak look at the Kid. Then he pitched forward, down the stairs. . . .

Judd's glance had centered on the saloon window. He saw the glass break and a muzzle thrust through, and his own Colt blasted first. The window shattered, and the man behind the muzzle cursed and staggered away.

Gary's first thought was that Yaegar was inside, that Sam Insted had been bait for an ambush. He was thinking this as he wheeled and caught the trailing reins of Jackson's gray. The animal

177

pulled away, dragging him around. . . . He let the gray go and sprinted for the stairs.

Judd was still throwing shots into Yaegar's, through the broken window. Behind Gary the Big Hat riders broke into the Square. They ranged up beside Judd, guns drawn. But there was no answering fire from the saloon.

Gary was by the door, gun cocked.

Someone inside Yaegar's was yelling: "Hold it, Big Hat! We've got enough!"

Gary looked at Judd. The sheriff shrugged.

"All right," Gary called sharply. "Come out. All of you!"

Keene and Hank Grogan came through the door. They were holding Baker. The ex-deputy's feet dragged, and his face was a pasty color. His right shoulder had been smashed by Judd's slug.

Frank Coons stepped out behind them, his hands high.

Gary motioned for them to range against the wall. "Toss your guns into the street!" he ordered.

They obeyed with sullen scowls. Keene spat through his teeth. He was looking down at Sam Insted's huddled body; he was remembering the Tombstone killer's boasting.

"Where's Yaegar?" Gary demanded.

Keene looked at his dispirited companions. Baker sagged suddenly, his face very white. His eyes rolled. Grogan caught him as he started to fall and eased him slowly down against the side of the building.

Gary repeated the question.

Keene shrugged. "He thought Sam could handle this. He went back to the ranch."

Gary turned to Judd. "How's the jail?"

"Let's take a look," Judd replied.

They crossed the Square. Keene and Hank Grogan carried Baker. Frank Coons went along, dragging his feet. Sam Insted's body lay where it had fallen.

The law office was as Judd had left it. No one had bothered to do anything about the debris. Judd surveyed the damage and made a visual inventory of his office. The two guns in the wall rack, a shotgun, 12 gauge, and a Winchester, Model '78, were gone . . . probably the work of petty thieves. The brass cuspidor that had been at his feet for twelve years was missing, too.

He stepped over the debris and pulled the door to the cell he had occupied wide open. "Put Baker on that cot," he ordered brusquely. He turned to Gary. "Send one of yore men for Tandy Mayling. She's Doc Jones' nurse when she ain't selling hats in the shop next door—"

The Diamond Cross men carried Baker to the cot and stood in uneasy silence. Judd made a sharp gesture with his gun. "You were happy as a calf on a teat when yore friends tore this down," he growled. "Let's get to work and clean up this mess!"

While they worked, Gary took the key ring from his pocket and tried to lock the remaining cell. But one section was twisted out of shape; the bolt end made no contact.

Judd said: "We'll lock it, Gary. If one of yore men will go down to Casey's Hardware and pick up a length of chain and a padlock, we'll be in business."

Gary dispatched Ollie Kemp on the mission. "Pick up a hammer, some six penny nails, a couple of hasps and two more padlocks," he told Kemp. "The rest of you dig up some boards. We're closing Yaegar's for good."

Judd overseed the cleaning up in his office, and when it was done to his satisfaction he herded the Diamond Cross men inside the cell. Tandy Mayling, a slender, bird-like woman in her thirties, came in with carbolic and bandages. She asked few questions. She did a neat job on Baker's shoulder.

After she had gone Judd used the chain and padlock to secure the cell door. The iron partition which had been ripped from the other cell had been righted into place, but it would take a blacksmith and a carpenter to fix it.

In the meantime Gary and his men had boarded the ground floor windows of Yaegar's Saloon and padlocked front and rear doors. Bill Tate had stopped by the paint shop and brush-painted a sign with crude but effective lettering:

CLOSED, By Order of the Sheriff's Office

Sam Insted's body was being taken to Moss Lake's funeral parlors when Judd came to join Gary.

"Have you seen Ann?" His voice was hesitant. He had been expecting his daughter to show up, but at the moment he didn't want to face her alone.

Gary shook his head. "I'll check at the hotel for her, Judd."

Judd nodded. "Gary, tell her I'm sorry—"

He turned away, and Gary watched him go back to the office, a small, wiry man who seemed even older than he had appeared this morning. Perhaps it was the way his shoulders sagged.

The Square was cleared again. It looked unchanged by the violence which had taken place less than an hour ago. Only the boarded windows in Yaegar's Saloon marked a difference.

Yaegar would probably be coming back. He had expected that Sam and the men he had left in town would be capable of taking care of any Big Hat move. But he'd be riding back to make sure.

Gary's lips curled. Time was a river that flowed one way; it didn't turn back, nor did it stop. And the time had come for a showdown with Diamond Cross, for the facing of Yaegar's guns.

He swung away, wanting to see Ann now. Wanting to tell her how he felt; wanting her to know that she was the real reason for his coming back to Del Rio.

The desk clerk shook his head at his request. "Mrs. Sigleman left yesterday. She did not return to the hotel last night."

Gary frowned. "She leave a message?"

"No message." The clerk hesitated. "I don't believe she intended to leave town, sir. She took no baggage with her. Nor did she check out at the desk."

"She didn't say where she was going?"

The man shook his head. "No, sir."

Gary walked out. The afternoon heat glared up from the street. He stood on the corner by the restaurant and rolled himself a smoke. Fear stirred in him. He remembered that Judd had said that Ann had gone to see him right after the jail break, while Yaegar's men were still in the Square. He thought of Ann and Yaegar, and the fear tightened in his belly and he felt his lips go dry.

The men Judd had jailed would know what had happened to Ann. If Yaegar had forced her to go with him—?

He stepped away from the corner and started across the Square. A wagon rumbled by, and he stopped to let it pass.

A moment later he threw up his hands and pitched forward. In the square a bullet made a flat, angry sound as it ricocheted off a cobblestone. . . . The crack of the distant rifle was unheard in the plaza.

CHAPTER XVII

Yaegar and his men rode into Big Hat at high noon. They missed Tony Armillo who was down by the river, putting wooden headboards over the two new graves. But they killed Ned Sewell when he stepped out of the blacksmith shed to investigate.

Larry Main and the cook returned the fire from the galley. The cook got a bullet through his leg, and Main wounded a Diamond Cross rider before he was killed.

Doc Jones stepped out of the ranchhouse door onto the porch, and a shot drew blood from his ear. Then Yaegar's hard voice silenced the Diamond Cross guns.

"Where's the rest of Big Hat?" Yaegar snarled. "Where's the Kid?"

Doc Jones leaned against the door. He felt sick. "Gone," he said. His voice held a bleak despair. "They rode to Del Rio. . . ."

Frustration put its harsh imprint on Yaegar's face. He had wanted to settle with Big Hat; the delay irked him. He looked around him, unconsciously comparing the size and the neatness of this spread with the hole-in-the-wall he occupied in the Blackrocks, and the urge was strong in him to burn this down to the ground, to take his revenge on Gary in this way. . . .

He stayed his hand. He had come across the border for Big Hat—it would do him little good to take over a gutted spread.

Texas Jack, the man on his right, broke into his thoughts. "Here comes Ozzie now. But Becker ain't with him—"

Yaegar turned impatiently. He had sent Ozzie back when Becker had failed to join them. Now, as he watched Ozzie's lathered mount pound toward them, a cold premonition of disaster touched his spine.

He rode to meet the man.

"Hell's broken loose!" Ozzie shouted. He pulled his spent mount to a dust-raising slide. His eyes still bugged in his head. "Diamond Cross's burned to the ground! Becker an' Reno are dead! So's that big hombre Becker had prisoner!"

"The girl?" Yaegar's voice was a whiplash.

"Joaquin said he saw her ride away. The Mexican was havin' his siesta by the spring when it happened. Couldn't get much out of him—but he said he saw the girl ride out—"

Yaegar cursed. Diamond Cross meant little to him; it had been no more than a temporary base of operations. Big Hat and the big house on the hill overlooking Del Rio were what he wanted— what he had crossed the Rio Grande for.

But now, as he thought of the Kid riding to town, a small doubt grew in him. Had Sam been able to stop the Kid?

If the Kid had outgunned Sam he'd be waiting in Del Rio. And the Kid was the only barrier between him and Big Hat.

He made his decision. He wheeled his big black toward the road to Del Rio. . . .

Ann Sigleman rode without direction that first hour. The horror of what she had witnessed made her sick; she clung limply to the horse's mane, shuddering, her eyes closed. The animal slackened his pace; there was no guidance from the woman in the saddle.

Ann finally recovered. She raised her head and looked back to Diamond Cross, but all she could see was a smudge of smoke rising against the blazing sky.

It took her another fifteen minutes to get her bearings; then she turned the animal toward town. She rode without thinking, feeling only a gray and dismal hopelessness. The ride to Del Rio seemed to last an eternity, to be a passage through limbo.

The Miller house, looming big and arrogant on the hill, jogged her into thinking. Henry Miller was Gary's uncle. He, too, had a stake in Big Hat. Perhaps he could muster help, if it was not already too late. . . .

She turned her mount up the road to the wide adobe archway and passed beneath it. A young Mexican attendant took her horse. She went to the iron-grill door, and Juan opened it for her, greeting her with a toothless smile.

It was then she heard a shot. A sharp sound, from somewhere on the second floor—the detonation of a rifle.

She stood rooted, chilled by a nameless fear. Juan turned and stared down the cool hallway. He was deaf as a post, but something in Ann's face alerted him.

Ann walked past him and turned into the library. Juan padded behind her; he stood in the doorway, his hands clasped in front of him, smiling. Ann turned to him.

"Where's Mister Miller, Juan?" She raised her voice; it seemed to ring through the still house.

"Right here, Ann," Henry said.

He was coming down the stairs, a regal-looking man, his hand extended in welcome. "What can I do for you? Is it about your father, Ann?"

She hesitated. "That shot? Are you all right, Mr. Miller?"

"Shot?" He seemed puzzled.

"Why, yes—" She made a swift gesture toward the stairs. "There was a shot, a rifle shot, I think, just as I came in. It sounded as if someone had fired a rifle upstairs—"

He took her hand and held it in his palm while

he patted it with the other. "My dear, I'm afraid you must have imagined it. I heard no shot." His face took on a look of concern. "You do seem overwrought. May I have Juan get you something?"

Ann slid her palm across her face. Her legs were trembling. Maybe she had imagined hearing a shot.

"Yes," she whispered. "Some sherry, please."

Miller turned to the old manservant and sent him for the sherry. He took her arm. "Please come in and sit down, Ann. I've seen so little of you these past years. When you were a little girl, in pigtails, you were a more constant visitor to this house."

He was pleasant and composed, and Ann thought, Are my nerves that bad? Could I have imagined I heard that rifle shot?

He led her to a chair. "What's troubling you, Ann? Your father?"

She nodded. She told him what had happened since Yaegar had forced her to accompany him to Diamond Cross. He listened, his face showing little emotion, little concern. Even as she talked Ann noticed this. . . . A sudden uneasiness brought back the echo of the rifle shot.

She got up and walked to the window and looked out. She could see down the slant of the hill to Del Rio's flat roof; she noticed now that she could see into the plaza. It occurred to her that from this window, and even more clearly from the window of the room above, Henry Miller could see almost everything that took place in Texas Square.

A knot of men were gathered around someone lying in the Square—she could see this, but not too clearly, for it was close to a thousand yards to the Square. Then the group seemed to break up, and she noticed men carrying a limp figure toward her father's office. And a small cry escaped her. One of those men was her father!

She turned swiftly and saw Henry Miller's eyes on her. They were dark and probing, and fear struck through her, whitening her lips.

"I don't think I'll wait for the sherry," she said. "Thank you for listening to me, Mr. Miller. I am overwrought. If you'll see me to the door—?"

He crossed in front of her and closed the door and put his back to it. "I'm sorry, Ann." His voice was smooth and cold, and it held no regret. "That view from the window disturbed you, didn't it?"

She looked at him, fighting a smothering feeling in her chest.

"The Castinados had a paternal feeling for Del Rio," Miller said. "They owned a thousand square miles of land. They must have felt they owned Del Rio, too. So they built this house on the hill, so they could watch over those below. An old European custom, you might say."

Ann barely recognized her voice. "Thank you for the information. But if you'll let me go now—"

"No, Ann!" Henry's voice was harsh now, stripped of politeness. "It's too bad you came at this moment, girl. The shot you heard, and the view from the window—I'm afraid you're too intelligent a girl not to understand what happened."

"I know nothing," the girl protested. "I saw a group of men around someone lying in the plaza. I don't even know who it was you—"

He chuckled softly. "I'll tell you, Ann. A high-powered rifle of German make and a telescopic sight are upstairs in my bedroom. And the man I killed is Gary Miller!"

She had been through too much today; her nerves were stretched too taut. Ann moaned softly and crumpled to the floor. . . .

Judd Vestry was coming into the Square when he saw men running toward Gary. He didn't recognize the Kid at first glance, and the press of the gathering, some of whom were Big Hat men, hid Gary from view.

Judd was coming from the Café Reale. He had gone there while Gary had looked for Ann at the hotel; he had taken Larry Main's advice. But Pedro had not needed the prodding of a gun muzzle to make him talk.

Not that Judd had not believed Gary. But

something in him had driven him to Pedro's, to find out what had happened that night. And now, as he came toward the group of men around Gary, he felt an inner peace, a release from the devils which had driven him.

He pushed through the men clustered around the Kid, and a shock went through him.

Bill Tate said: "He was walking toward the office, Judd, when it happened. I didn't hear the shot. . . ."

Judd knelt by the Kid. Relief softened the harshness of his features as he saw that the bullet had only creased Gary. He had an ugly-looking gash just over his right ear; it looked worse than it was. Even as he touched the area around the cut, Gary stirred. A tight moan came through the Kid's teeth.

"Get him into my office!" Judd snapped.

He turned and searched the building line as Bill Tate and Art Lord picked the Kid up. One of Yaegar's men, with a rifle? One man? It didn't make sense.

His eyes lifted above the building line to the big Miller house on the hill. A small frown came to groove a deep line between his eyes.

He followed the straggle of men to the office. Gary had recovered consciousness. He sat in a chair and leaned his head back against the wall. Bill Tate was wiping the blood from Gary's face.

Judd crouched beside the Kid. "Where's Ann?"

Gary looked at him. "Gone." His voice was thin. "Left the hotel yesterday. She didn't come back last night!"

Judd's face turned gray. "Yaegar?"

Gary tried to get to his feet. He motioned to the prisoners in the cell. "Ask them, Judd."

Judd straightened. He said softly: "If Ann's at Diamond Cross, I'll—"

Ollie Kemp came through the door, stepping fast. "Yaegar! Coming up Main Street. He's got six men with him, Judd!"

The sheriff looked at Gary. The Kid sucked in a harsh breath and pushed Bill Tate's hand aside. He stood up and put a hand against the wall to steady himself.

"This is the showdown, Judd. This is the way it has to be. . . ."

CHAPTER XVIII

Yaegar rode into Del Rio with his men flanking him. He came around the corner into Texas Square, a tall, alert man whose reputation reached a long way from the Mexican border.

He sensed something was wrong almost immediately, even before he saw the small cluster of men break and scatter away from the sheriff's office . . . before his roving glance picked up the two Big Hat men lounging under the arcade two doors down from his saloon.

The boarded windows were a shock. . . . Yaegar turned the big black toward the saloon and read the sign nailed across the padlocked door.

Yaegar edged his black around and faced the Big Hat men under the arcade. His voice held a stony challenge.

"So Sam wasn't good enough?"

Al Smith, youngest of the Big Hat riders, shuffled nervously. Nixon, a stocky older man, answered: "Sam's dead."

"And the Kid?"

Nixon's glance lifted. "Right behind you, Yaegar. Waiting for you."

Yaegar didn't move at first. He sensed panic rustle through the men flanking him, heard the creak of saddle leather, the sound of a muttered, frightened curse. Contempt flickered briefly in his eyes. These men would fold up the minute things went wrong. He knew this, sensing it with quick intuition.

He backed the black stallion around and got a look at the Kid. And at Judd. But it was the Kid he measured and weighed.

A lean, rangy fellow with a cat's quick reflexes. A good-looking youngster, despite the blood-stained handkerchief knotted around his head, the stubble on his face. A hard man to beat. . . .

He measured the Kid, and a knot formed in the pit of his stomach, and then a cold smile edged his lips.

All trails end somewhere, Doc had said. And looking at the Kid, Yaegar had a momentary sense of unreality, as though this cobbled plaza, hot in the waning afternoon, were a figment of a dream. It was not a place to die, he thought, and he had to stifle an impulse to look around, to see if the rest of Del Rio was still there.

"Where's Ann?" It was the Kid's voice, cold and bitter, that reached up to Yaegar.

Yaegar's gaze touched briefly the men edging up behind the Kid and Judd. Then he put his attention on Gary, and his voice held a naked hate. "In hell, I hope."

Judd drew first. His hand was on his Colt butt when Yaegar cut down at him. The gun boss's bullet spun Judd around. . . . His second grazed Gary's neck. Then Yaegar straightened in the saddle, the shock of Gary's slugs lifting him. He was dimly aware of other shots and knew that his men were milling around him. Then he felt himself falling. The last person he saw was the Kid, still standing, his crouched lean body half hidden by gunsmoke.

Then for Yaegar, too, the trail had come to its ending!

With Yaegar down, the fight swiftly ebbed from the remaining Diamond Cross riders. Two had joined Yaegar on the cobbles. The others dropped their guns and raised their hands in quick surrender.

Gary turned to Judd. The man had taken Yaegar's slug in the right shoulder.

"Ann!" he said through clenched teeth. "Find her, Gary. . . ."

The Kid nodded. He walked to the nearest Diamond Cross man, and his fingers closed over the man's shirt front. "Where's Ann Sigleman?" His voice held a savage fury. "What happened to her?"

"She's alive. That's all I know," Ozzie said. He shrank from the blaze in the Kid's eyes. "It's the truth! Diamond Cross is burned out." He recited what he knew, and what Joaquin had told him.

Relief flooded through Gary. Ann was safe; she would be showing up in town soon. He went back to Judd. "Ann's all right," he reassured Vestry. "Don't worry about her. Have Tandy take care of that shoulder until Doc gets in from the ranch. I'll see you later."

"Where you headed?"

"To see a man about a bill for ten thousand dollars," the Kid answered cryptically.

The Miller house stood out boldly under the rays of the afternoon sun. It was a house strongly built of heavy timbers and thick adobe. It was a house that had never been home to Gary Miller. But it was a place with which he was intimately familiar.

Juan met him at the door and showed him to the library and retired on silent feet, a senile old man, smiling vacuously.

"Come in," Henry Miller said pleasantly. "I've been expecting you, Gary!"

He was standing by the window, behind the chair on which Ann sat—sat rigidly, her face white, her eyes dark with fear.

The .32 revolver in Henry Miller's right hand was against Ann's neck!

Gary froze.

"Come in," Henry invited. "Sit down. . . ."

Gary didn't move. He had not expected to find Ann here, nor was he prepared for this.

"They're all dead, aren't they?" his uncle said. "The men on that list I gave you?"

Gary nodded. He was eyeing the muzzle of Henry's gun, pressed against Ann's neck, and he felt sick.

"All of them," he muttered. "All except one. Me. I wasn't on that list. Nor were Doc and Jackson. But we were on your list, weren't we?"

Henry Miller shrugged. "As long as you were alive, Big Hat belonged to you, Gary. I couldn't risk that. I couldn't live with the thought that some day you might come back and take it from me. Neither you nor my brother really appreciated this house. Your father thought only of cows. And you, Gary—you were never anything but a wild kid!"

"Then it was you who killed my father?"

"No one will ever prove that," Miller said. "But he threatened to throw me out when he learned I had talked Salters into selling out to Yaegar. He accused me of bringing Yaegar into Del Rio, of hiring Yaegar to make trouble for Big Hat."

"He was right, wasn't he?" Gary was inching toward Miller, hoping for some diversion that would throw the man off guard.

"Of course. Yaegar readily accepted my proposition." Miller laughed softly. "He believed me when I told him he'd have Big Hat while I wanted only this big house. Or perhaps he didn't really believe me. I think he planned to take everything, once you were out of the way."

Gary frowned. "You knew I was coming?"

"I knew you'd come back." Miller nodded. "That's why I brought Yaegar to Del Rio. When your father was killed, it was natural for people to believe that Yaegar, or one of Yaegar's men, had killed him." He shook his head slightly. "That's far enough, Gary. Believe me, any slight motion on your part, and I will kill her!"

Gary came down off his toes. "You'll hang!" he muttered.

"I doubt it," Miller said. "I've planned this a long time, Gary. I kept track of you for years. I knew you were the Kid. A formidable character." He sneered. "So I picked Yaegar, whose reputation rivaled yours. His job was to kill you."

"What would it have gained you?" Gary asked harshly. "You would have had Yaegar to deal with—"

"You underestimate me, Gary—you always have. When the law made its investigation here, as it eventually would, Yaegar, if he was still alive, would be thrown to the wolves. But I had faith in you and your friends. I knew Yaegar would not escape unscathed."

"One faction against the other," Gary said softly. "And now you have only me to dispose of?"

"I thought I had, earlier this afternoon," Miller said. "But I'm afraid I'm not as good a shot with the German Manliccher as I supposed."

Gary looked at Ann, and Miller added: "She

paid me a visit at the wrong time, Gary. She heard the rifle shot and she had a look out the window. I realized then she knew. I couldn't let her go—"

"What do you want?" Gary grated.

"Everything that is rightfully yours," Miller said coolly. "This house—and Big Hat."

"You could have had them," Gary told him. "I never intended to stay—"

"Perhaps," Miller interrupted skeptically. "But this is a surer way." He gave a slight tilt of his head. "There's a paper on my desk for you to sign. Sign it, Gary, and you and Ann can go. I'll even give you a wedding present: a draft for five thousand dollars."

Gary put his gaze on Ann. She was trying to tell him something with her eyes—something he couldn't understand.

"You'll let us go free?"

"Sign the paper," Miller urged softly.

The man was lying. Henry would never let him walk out of there alive, Gary knew. Uncle Henry could never be sure that Gary wouldn't come back. . . . And this, the Kid knew, was the reason Miller would kill him.

He walked to the desk and looked down at the closely written document. For the consideration of five thousand dollars, it read, Gary Miller turned over to his uncle all properties accruing to him from his father's death.

"Sign it," Miller ordered. He was looking at

Gary now, and not at Ann, and it was then that Gary understood what Ann was going to do.

He picked up the quill pen and bent over the paper and the quill slipped through his fingers. It provided the slight diversion of attention he hoped for, and Ann took advantage of it. She flung herself sideways, out of the chair, to the floor. . . .

Henry Miller fired by reflex. The sharp bark of the .32 was lost in the heavier explosions from Gary's gun. Miller never clearly realized what happened. He felt a burst of pain, and that was all.

Gary walked to Ann and lifted her to her feet, and Ann clung to him, sobbing softly. . . .

Del Rio dozes in the sun. The fountain in Texas Square murmurs softly, its peaceful sound underscoring the cries of playing children.

Judd Vestry sits in a chair in front of the rebuilt law office. The star on his vest is a symbol. He knows he can count on Big Hat in an emergency—but there is no emergency in Del Rio.

Tom Blake runs Big Hat and raises Herefords, and Gary and Ann Miller often spend time there. But the old Castinado house on the hill is where they live.

And to Gary Miller, it is now home!

Center Point Large Print
600 Brooks Road / PO Box 1
Thorndike, ME 04986-0001 USA

(207) 568-3717

US & Canada:
1 800 929-9108
www.centerpointlargeprint.com